W9-CCQ-550

Josie had been wrong about being prepared to see Del again.

Especially after three long years and her endless, agonizing reconstructive surgeries and rehabilitation.

Recognition slammed into her. Her chest went tight, and her legs shook as she stared at the man who'd once been her husband.

Del was tall, broad shouldered, his muscles earned through years of construction work. His dark hair gleamed in the overhead lights, and his eyes were still chocolate-brown and glinting with humor. He was good-looking, charming and, she knew from experience, *very* attentive in bed.

He was also staring at her with the polite expression he would offer any stranger.

"I'm Delaney Scott," he said, holding out his hand. "How can I help you?"

Josie blinked in surprise. Del didn't recognize her.

While seeing him again had rocked her to her soul....

Dear Reader,

While every romance holds the promise of sweeping readers away with a rugged alpha male or a charismatic cowboy, this month we want to take a closer look at the women who fall in love with our favorite heroes.

"Heroines need to be strong," says Sherryl Woods, author of more than fifty novels. "Readers look for a woman who can stand up to the hero—and stand up to life." Sherryl's book *A Love Beyond Words* features a special heroine who lost her hearing but became stronger because of it. "A heroine needs to triumph over fear or adversity."

Kate Stockwell faces the fear of knowing she cannot bear her own child in Allison Leigh's *Her Unforgettable Fiancé,* the next installment in the STOCKWELLS OF TEXAS miniseries. And an accident forces Josie Scott, Susan Mallery's LONE STAR CANYON heroine in *Wife in Disguise,* to take stock of her life and find a second chance....

In Peggy Webb's *Standing Bear's Surrender,* Sarah Sloan must choose between loyalty and true love! In *Separate Bedrooms...?* by Carole Halston, Cara LaCroix is faced with fulfilling her grandmother's final wish—marriage! And Kirsten Laurence needs the help of the man who broke her heart years ago in Laurie Campbell's *Home at Last.*

"A heroine is a real role model," Sherryl says. And in Special Edition, we aim for every heroine to be a woman we can all admire. Here's to strong women and many more emotionally satisfying reads from Silhouette Special Edition!

Karen Taylor Richman
Senior Editor

Please address questions and book requests to:
Silhouette Reader Service
U.S.: 3010 Walden Ave., P.O. Box 1325, Buffalo, NY 14269
Canadian: P.O. Box 609, Fort Erie, Ont. L2A 5X3

Wife in Disguise

SUSAN MALLERY

Silhouette®

SPECIAL EDITION™

Published by Silhouette Books

America's Publisher of Contemporary Romance

If you purchased this book without a cover you should be aware that this book is stolen property. It was reported as "unsold and destroyed" to the publisher, and neither the author nor the publisher has received any payment for this "stripped book."

To those who have survived the trials of life,
while coming through the fire
with grace and humor intact.

SILHOUETTE BOOKS

ISBN 0-373-24383-9

WIFE IN DISGUISE

Copyright © 2001 by Susan Macias Redmond

All rights reserved. Except for use in any review, the reproduction or utilization of this work in whole or in part in any form by any electronic, mechanical or other means, now known or hereafter invented, including xerography, photocopying and recording, or in any information storage or retrieval system, is forbidden without the written permission of the editorial office, Silhouette Books, 300 East 42nd Street, New York, NY 10017 U.S.A.

All characters in this book have no existence outside the imagination of the author and have no relation whatsoever to anyone bearing the same name or names. They are not even distantly inspired by any individual known or unknown to the author, and all incidents are pure invention.

This edition published by arrangement with Harlequin Books S.A.

® and TM are trademarks of Harlequin Books S.A., used under license. Trademarks indicated with ® are registered in the United States Patent and Trademark Office, the Canadian Trade Marks Office and in other countries.

Visit Silhouette at www.eHarlequin.com

Printed in U.S.A.

SUSAN MALLERY

is the bestselling author of over thirty-five books for Silhouette. Always a fan of romance novels, Susan finds herself in the unique position of living out her own personal romantic fantasy with the new man in her life. Susan lives in Washington State with her handsome hero husband and her two adorable-but-not-bright cats.

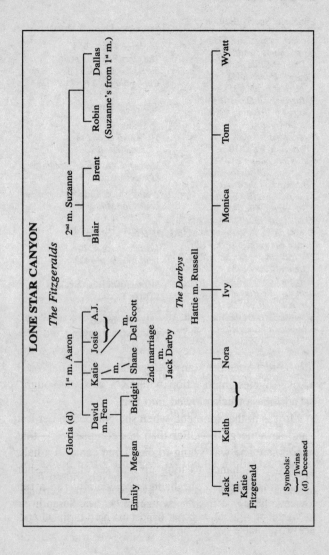

LONE STAR CANYON

The Fitzgeralds

Gloria (d)   1st m. Aaron   2nd m. Suzanne

Blair   Brent   Robin   Dallas
(Suzanne's from 1st m.)

David   Katie   Josie   A.J.
m. Fern   m.
                Shane Del Scott

Emily Megan Bridgit

2nd marriage
m.
Jack Darby

The Darbys

Hattie m. Russell

Jack   Keith   Nora   Ivy   Monica   Tom   Wyatt
m.
Katie
Fitzgerald

Symbols:
⁀ Twins
(d) Deceased

Prologue

The accident occurred in slow motion.

One minute Josie Fitzgerald Scott was driving home for lunch as she did most days, the next, her life changed forever. There was no warning, no premonition that this Tuesday at 11:45 a.m. was going to be different from any other. She entered the West Los Angeles intersection without a second thought. And then a truck plowed into her.

It was at that moment, when she glanced to her left and saw the grill—taller than her compact car—that she knew she was going to die. Time came to a halt. She had a chance to look up and see that yes, her light *was* green so she hadn't accidentally run a red by mistake. She briefly thought about accelerating or braking, to lessen the impact of the impending collision. But before she could decide, the truck was on her and the first sickening sound of metal on metal filled her ears.

Mercifully, she felt nothing. Not pressure, not pain, not even panic. As she was thrust to her right by the force of the truck slamming into her car, she wondered what she would regret as she breathed her last. Would it be her tacit estrangement from her family or her solitary existence? Would it be...

The sound increased until it filled her head. She had an odd sensation of being disconnected from her body, of not actually being a part of the destruction. She heard screams and vaguely wondered if they were her own.

Then the darkness beckoned. But before she could step into the waiting oblivion, she felt her first and only regret. Del. That she would never see him again or tell him that she was sorry for everything that had gone wrong between them.

As her car was crushed like a soda can, breaking her body and ravaging her face, she slipped into the blackness. With her last conscious thought, she breathed the name of the man who had once wanted her for his own.

Chapter One

One year later

The old Miller place was for sale. Josie Scott parked her Volvo in front of the old Victorian mansion and stared at the gabled roof line. She'd been fighting nothing but memories since she'd driven into Beachside Bay, California, earlier that morning, and seeing the old house only made the problem worse. She'd returned to town for closure, but what she was getting instead was a quick course in how to survive a brutal trip down memory lane.

"I'm on a mission," she reminded herself. A mission that should take two, maybe three days at most. Then she would leave the land of her past and return to...

Actually she didn't have anything to return to, but

this wasn't the time to remember that. Better to focus on the past and why she was here. So she looked at the Miller house and remembered when she and Del had visited it, one of the many times it had been on the market.

"We could rip out the entire third floor and make it into a master suite," he'd said one Saturday long ago. They'd been standing at the top of the narrow staircase leading to the unused third floor of the mansion. "New bathroom, sitting area, even a study."

Josie had planted her hands on her jeans-clad hips and stubbornly shaken her head. "It'll be too hot."

Del turned to her, his dark eyes glinting with laughter. "There's this new invention. Maybe you've heard of it. Air-conditioning? The master suite could have its own unit."

She hadn't been convinced. "I want the master on the second floor."

"Where will the kids sleep?"

She'd rolled her eyes, then turned away, tucking a strand of short blond hair behind her ear. She hadn't been about to get trapped in *that* discussion again. Del wanted kids; she wasn't ready. He wanted the master up, she wanted it down. He wanted her home and cooking dinner and she wanted a career. They hadn't agreed on the Miller house, nor on anything else of importance.

Josie leaned back in the front seat of her car and closed her eyes. "Oh, Del, what were we thinking?" Their three-year marriage had been one long argument punctuated by great sex. In fact, they'd currently been divorced as long as they'd been married. So what on earth was she doing in Beachside Bay?

"Closure," she murmured to herself, opening her eyes and starting her car engine.

Yes, she and Del were divorced. From what she'd heard, while he hadn't remarried he'd certainly moved on with his life. She had, too, or so she'd thought until her accident a year before. Del had been her last thought before she'd slipped into unconsciousness and her first thought upon waking in the hospital. He'd been on her mind on and off through the past twelve months of surgery, physical therapy and more surgery. Obviously, she wasn't as over him as she'd thought.

So here she was, back where the trouble had begun. All she wanted was a couple of quick conversations with her ex so that she could put her past behind her. A simple plan, but one that wasn't going to work if she didn't have the courage to go talk to him.

"So do it now," she ordered herself as she slipped the car into gear, checked the mirrors and road ahead before pulling out onto the quiet side street.

She drove the scant three miles to the offices of Scott Construction. As she did she was assaulted by memories of living in the sleepy seaside town. Beachside Bay was directly west of San Jose but light years from anything remotely resembling a burgeoning economy. The main residents were college kids and retirees who actually existed in peaceful acceptance. Funky restaurants and elegant bed and breakfasts pulled in the vacation crowd, but there wasn't enough industry to keep the tourists longer than a weekend or two a year.

She turned the corner and pulled into the parking lot of Scott Construction. The low one-story building still looked more like a beach house than an office.

Flowers, mostly roses, bloomed along the edges of the parking lot and up the long walkway.

Memories assaulted her. She remembered how the place had looked when she'd been all of nineteen and looking for a part-time job. The twenty-five hours a week of light office work had been more than enough to supplement her athletic scholarship. The fact that the Scotts' son was three years her senior, good-looking enough to have his own beefcake calendar and a charmer to boot had simply been a bonus.

But all the memories weren't so fun, Josie admitted to herself. She could also recall the times when she and Del had been fighting. He'd left for work, but she hadn't been content to let things rest. Instead she'd followed him to the office to continue screaming at him, not caring who heard or what they thought of her.

She gripped the steering wheel, squeezing tightly and trying to erase that part of her past. She had many things to atone for. She'd been unprepared for marriage, with the sensibilities of a spoiled teenager rather than a grown woman. Would Del be interested in listening to her say that now, or had he put her so far behind him that it didn't matter anymore? There was only one way to find out.

Gathering her courage, Josie turned off the engine and carefully put the keys into her purse. As she opened the door of her sedan, she shifted her weight so that she could turn to face out. She swung her legs slowly and painfully around until her feet touched the ground. When she was ready, she braced one hand on the specially installed handle by the back of her seat and pushed into a standing position. Her leg muscles—especially those in her left leg—quivered and threatened to give way. She forced herself to remain completely still until she'd achieved her balance. Only then did she turn and bend down so she could pull out her purse and her cane.

For one brief moment in time she allowed herself to remember what it had been like when she'd taken her body for granted. She'd been a born athlete and her world had consisted of running and bounding and achieving. Over the past year she'd learned to measure her progress in single steps...sometimes in mere inches.

She draped her purse over her right shoulder and braced the cane with her left hand. The path up to the building seemed endlessly long, with three shallow steps in the ten or so feet of concrete. There was a time when she would have raced to the door without a second thought. Now she had to consciously move her damaged left leg, lifting with still-healing muscles and ignoring the burning pain that was her constant companion. She paused at the halfway point to catch her breath and to admire Catherine's exquisite roses.

Del's mother had a gift for making things grow. The mild temperatures had brought the fragrant blooms out early, and Josie lingered to inhale their sweetness. When she was relaxed and rested enough to continue, she started for the glass door.

As she moved, she could see herself reflected in the glass. The tall, awkwardly gaited woman was a stranger. Not just the long hair and the soft flowing dress, but the face. The side impact of the truck had caused glass to slice her face. In the first six months after the accident, a gifted plastic surgeon had restored the damage, making her into a pretty young woman. But the slightly more prominent cheekbones and rounded chin had little in common with the features of her birth. Except for her eyes and the shape of her mouth, she was a stranger to herself. She smiled as she thought of Del's shock as he would try to figure out who she was, then his reaction when he did. Her smile faded. Would he be happy or annoyed that she'd walked back into his life?

She reached the glass door and managed to maneuver her way into the waiting area of the office. The spacious entry had been filled with large windows and comfortable furniture. Oversize photos of recent restorations hung on the wall. A rectangular table in the center offered a place to study blueprints.

Josie turned to the receptionist, sitting behind a big cherry-wood desk. The dark-haired woman in her late forties didn't look familiar. She offered Josie a pleasant smile.

"May I help you?"

Josie had to brush her suddenly damp palms against her skirt. She could feel her stomach tightening as she fought against the need to flee. She'd been crazy to come back. Del wasn't going to want to talk to her. They'd been divorced for three years; they had nothing to say to each other.

"I, um…" She cleared her throat. The accident had damaged her vocal cords so that her normally high-pitched voice had become low and husky. "I'd like to see Del Scott, please. I don't have an appointment."

The woman nodded. "He just happens to be in. Let me buzz him." She paused. "I'm sorry. I didn't get your name."

Before Josie could respond, the phone rang. The woman excused herself and took the call. Three more followed in rapid succession. When there was a lull, she quickly buzzed Del and told him he had a visitor.

Josie limped over to a sofa and studied the floral print. She was more concerned about the softness of the padding than the fabric used. If she sat down, she wanted to be sure that she could stand up again. Getting trapped in a chair wasn't her idea of making a good impression on her ex.

The door leading to the back swung open. Josie turned quickly—too quickly. Her weight shifted before her legs were ready and she nearly stumbled. Only by putting most of her weight on her cane was she able to stay upright. She forced herself to get control and balance before she allowed herself to look at the newcomer.

She'd been wrong about being prepared to see him again.

Recognition slammed into her. Her chest went tight and her leg muscles shook the way they did after a ninety-minute therapy session. Sound seemed to fade, then get too loud as she stared at the man who'd once been her husband.

Del was tall—six foot two—which made him about a half foot taller than her. He was broad shouldered with muscles earned through years of construction work. Close-cropped dark hair gleamed in the overhead lights and his eyes were still chocolate-brown and glinting with humor. He was good-looking, charming and attentive in bed.

He was also staring at her with the polite expression he would offer any stranger.

"I'm Delaney Scott," he said, holding out his hand. "Please call me Del. How can I help you?"

He didn't recognize her. Josie blinked in surprise.

She'd thought it might take him a minute, but she'd never considered the fact that he wouldn't even have a flicker of recognition.

"I, um…"

Her voice trailed off as she struggled to figure out what she was supposed to say. Seeing him had rocked her to her soul. As she continued to stare at his familiar features, she realized that she didn't know what she was feeling. Confusion, a draw to the past, a strong desire to run. What on earth had she been thinking when she'd come here? Was she going to say, "Gee, Del, I'm Josie. Can we talk about what went wrong in our marriage?" She needed time. The trick was how to get some.

Finally she realized he was still holding out his hand. She offered hers and they shook. The feel of his skin against hers was too familiar. She shivered as she remembered all the wonderful things that hand could do to her.

As she released him, she was conscious of his questioning silence and the stare of the receptionist. Josie wasn't talking, she wasn't doing anything but acting like an idiot. If she wasn't careful they were going to call for the men with the straitjackets.

Del motioned to the sofa she'd been studying. "Would you like a seat?"

She tapped her cane lightly on the hardwood floor. "I'm a little concerned about being able to get up if I do."

As she spoke the words, she kept her gaze on his face, wanting to see any revulsion or pity in his expression. Neither appeared. Instead he glanced at the couch, then nodded. "Why don't you risk it? If there's a problem when we're done, I'll help you up. Or Jan will." He nodded at the receptionist.

"All right."

Josie shifted until she was standing in front of the sofa, then slowly lowered herself into a sitting position. She hated that she had to think the process through—keeping her weight evenly distributed and using her cane to slow her descent. Nothing physical was easy for her anymore.

Del settled at the far end of the couch and angled toward her. His expression was pleasant, if slightly confused. He still had no clue who she was.

"Do you want to tell me why you stopped by?" he asked, with the patience of someone dealing with a very shy person. "I assume it has something to do with a house. Are you interested in restoration?"

Just being this close to him made her feel safe. Josie realized that she'd spent the past twelve months fighting fear. The relief of being able to let it go— even for a few minutes—made her feel giddy enough to float.

As she looked into his dark eyes, she realized that she'd been insane to expect Del to simply take a meeting with her and discuss their marriage. It had been three years. They were strangers. He wouldn't care that she needed closure.

But she also wasn't willing to walk away. The last year of their marriage had been hell. One fight after another, punctuated by periods of rage. Which meant she should have been over him. Yet ever since the accident, she hadn't been able to get Del out of her mind. She needed time to figure out why. There seemed to be only one way to get that respite.

"I'm interested in the Miller place," she said, surprising both him and herself.

He raised his dark eyebrows. "It's a beautiful home, but it will require extensive remodeling. We're talking about a lot of time and money."

Thanks to her injuries and a settlement from the company that owned the truck that hit her, she had plenty of both. "I'm not an expert on old houses," she said, "but I don't expect it to be easy. Is this the sort of project you'd be willing to take on?"

Interest brightened his eyes, and he grinned. "I've been admiring that old place for years. In fact I have some plans that I drew up a long time ago."

He spoke the words casually, as if they had no meaning. But they made Josie want to run away. She knew exactly when he'd drawn up the plans. It had been during the last year of their marriage, when they had almost had enough money to buy the old place. But it had quickly become obvious to both of them that they didn't have a prayer of agreeing on anything about the project.

"If you're interested, I can show them to you," he told her. "It would be easier at the house where I can show you what I'm talking about."

She nodded her agreement. "That sounds lovely. I, um, suppose we should make an appointment."

He rose and walked over to the receptionist's desk. After grabbing her scheduling calendar, he flipped the page to glance at the rest of the week. "I have some time tomorrow. Does that suit you?"

Josie swallowed. Did she really plan to go through with this? Was she going to buy the old Miller place and have Del renovate it for her? Shouldn't she just tell him who she was so they could talk and then she could go about her business?

Except she didn't have any business, personal or otherwise. Until her next surgery, her entire life consisted of healing from the last one. She didn't have a permanent home anymore or a job. Restoring the house would give her something to look forward to and be a part of. If nothing else, she could consider it an investment. When she was finished, she could always sell at a profit. Old restored Victorians were all the rage, even in Beachside Bay.

"Tomorrow is fine."

They settled on a time. Suddenly eager to escape, she braced her weight on her cane and slowly stood. With Del solicitously holding open the door, she made her painful way to the exit.

When she was about to step outside, she paused to look at him. She knew every inch of his face and body, but he hadn't recognized her. Not that she blamed him. Not only was her face completely different, but her shape had changed as well. Gone were the lean lines from her aggressive exercise program. She'd gained weight in the past year, filling out in her breasts and hips. Her legs bore scars, especially the left one. If he could see under the flowing folds of her floral print dress, he would be shocked...and repulsed.

"Thanks, Del," she said in her throaty voice. "I'm looking forward to hearing what you think you can do with the house."

"Me, too." He smiled, then his mouth straightened and he stiffened. "I'm sorry. I just realized I never caught your name."

She opened her mouth to tell him the truth, then

pressed her lips together. She wasn't ready to make explanations. She needed more time. A light breeze stirred her hair. It brought with it the scent of the beautiful flowers blooming in the warm spring afternoon. She glanced at his mother's garden and then returned her attention to him.

"I'm Rose."

The statement came from nowhere, but she didn't take it back. Instead she started walking before he could ask her for a last name. She would have to come up with one tonight.

"See you tomorrow," he called after her.

She waved without looking back. She didn't want to know that he was watching her, studying her slow steps, probably wondering what was wrong with her. She made it to her car without incident and sank onto the firm seat. With him still looking on, she backed out of the parking lot.

As she drove away, she was both desperate to know what he'd thought of her and grateful she couldn't begin to guess. She was nothing like the woman he remembered as Josie Fitzgerald Scott. On the one hand, he'd divorced that Josie, so he couldn't have cared about her too much. Of course he'd also married her, so there had been some kind of attraction and affection between them.

Josie turned left at the stop sign, then headed for the real estate office. If she was going to have her ex-husband restore the Miller Victorian house, then she'd better see about buying it. At least the old place had been vacant for years. That, combined with her ability to pay cash for the place, would mean that she could have a quick escrow.

Had she done the right thing, she wondered as she

drove, or was she crazy? Pretending to be someone else sure wasn't smart. Maybe she should have just told Del the truth about herself. But she hated the thought of seeing the pity and shock in his eyes. Better for him to think of her as a stranger. All she needed was a little time to get to know him again. Once they were friends, she would confess all and then convince him to talk about their marriage enough to give her closure. After that, she would be free to get on with her life. Free to figure out who she was and what she was going to do, now that everything she'd loved about herself was gone.

Chapter Two

Del Scott climbed the front steps of the old Miller place. It was nearly eleven in the morning on the kind of day designed to make every person not living in Beachside Bay want to sell their house, pack up their belongings and move to the oceanside town. The sky was a perfect California blue, the temperatures promised to reach into the mid-seventies and a faint tang of salt scented the sweet breeze.

Del paused to study the porch and front door of the old place. Both were in need of repainting, but the structure was fundamentally sound. He'd been through the house enough times to be able to picture every room and imagine the possibilities. At one time he'd even thought he might live here. The plans he'd brought along with him were proof of that. That dream had disappeared along with his wife. Although he could regret losing the house he could honestly say that he didn't have the same feelings about Josie. She was out of his life forever, and he was glad.

As he raised his hand to knock on the front door, he frowned. He hadn't thought about his ex-wife in months. Maybe not in the past year. Why had she turned up in his mind now? Was it being back at the Miller place? After all, they'd often talked about buying it. But every time they'd toured it, they'd ended up arguing about remodeling, just like they'd argued about everything else.

Forget it, he told himself firmly as he knocked.

As he waited for a response, he listened for the slow step of the soon-to-be owner. Rose. He frowned as he realized she hadn't given him a last name. She'd intrigued him, which was strange. They'd exchanged only a handful of words. Maybe it had been the way the light had caught her pale-blond hair. Josie's hair had been that color, but she'd always worn it as short as a boy, while Rose had soft, feminine waves that slipped down to her shoulders. With her big blue eyes and full mouth, she reminded him of a 1940s movie star. Curvy, sultry and a dozen kinds of trouble.

Before he could tell himself that sexual attraction to a client was a serious mistake, the front door opened. If he'd been hoping that seeing his potential new customer in person would erase the image he had of her as a temptress, he'd been mistaken.

Yesterday she'd worn a light-green dress. Today's was pink. Short sleeves in a gauzy material flirted with her upper arms. The floral print fabric skimmed over full breasts and hips before falling gently to her calves. Makeup accentuated her big eyes and full mouth, and the fact that she was leaning heavily on a cane did nothing to stem his male interest.

"Good morning," he said, forcing his voice to sound professional rather than husky with yearning. What on earth was wrong with him? He'd given up unrealized crushes on women about the time he'd turned seventeen and Betty Jo Lancaster had let him go all the way in the backseat of his Mustang.

"Mr. Scott." She gave him a brief nod and a quick smile. "You're very prompt. I appreciate that."

"Just part of the Scott family service. We're on time and we come prepared to do work. The same applies to my crew. If I tell you they'll be starting at eight, they'll all be here then. And please, call me Del."

"All right. Del." She stepped back to let him into the vacant house.

A beautiful chandelier hung in the foyer. He knew that it and the marble tiles underfoot had been shipped over from Italy in the early 1920s.

"I've been reacquainting myself with the house," Rose said, closing the door behind him and turning slowly toward the main living area, keeping her cane close to her side. "I'd forgotten how much work the house needs."

He was surprised to experience a stab of disappointment. He told himself his feelings came from having wanted to fix the old place for the past ten years, not from the realization that Rose might drift out of his life as easily as she'd drifted into it.

"Have you changed your mind about the remodeling?"

"Not at all. I'm prepared to see her looking as lovely as she did when she was first built."

Her comment surprised him. "Have you seen pictures?"

"A long time ago."

Before he could ask when, she started through the foyer, pointing to the front parlor. "I thought that room could be a combination living room and library. What do you think about bookshelves on a couple of the walls?"

He tapped the large case he carried. "You read my mind. I already have that design drawn up. Which leaves this as the main living area."

They stepped into an oversize room about twenty-five by thirty. The ten-foot ceilings and crown molding added to the grandeur of the room. The hardwood floors were in need of refinishing but otherwise in good shape. On the right, bay windows let in morning light. To the left was the entry to the kitchen and dining room. A huge fireplace dominated the north wall.

Del pointed at the bricked opening. "That was imported from a castle in England. The stained glass in the dining room came from a château in France. There are bits and pieces of the world all over the house."

"That's one of the things that intrigues me about the place," Rose told him. She paused in the center of the room, leaning heavily on her cane. "I don't agree with the current construction philosophy that if it's new it must be better. Sometimes what's old has a unique charm that can't be duplicated."

"I agree."

He noticed that her movements were slow and deliberate, the way they'd been the day before. He wondered if her disability was new—the result of an accident—or if she'd been born with it.

He grabbed a couple of straight-back chairs tucked in a corner of the room. There was also a folding table, flattened and leaning against the wall opposite the fireplace.

"Have a seat," he said, putting the chairs in the center of the room, then retrieving the table. "Let me show you my plans."

She settled into the chair and smiled at him. "You noticed me weaving. I'm a little tired, which always affects my balance."

"Actually I didn't," he said, and it was almost the truth. "My mom raised me to offer a lady a seat. This is the best I can do under the circumstances."

He straightened the table legs and locked them into place. After placing it in front of the two chairs, he opened his large briefcase.

"What do you know about the house?" he asked. "Any of the history?"

She shook her head. As she moved, the long, blond strands swayed back and forth, the gentle wave causing a curve of her hair to brush her cheek. He was once again reminded of a forties movie star…and his ex-wife, which was a strange combination. It was the hair color, he told himself. And the eye color. They were startlingly similar. But Rose and Josie had little else in common. Rose was quiet, elegant and feminine. Josie had been an argumentative whirlwind. Not exactly restful.

He opened his case and slid out the large sheets of paper, then set them on the table. But instead of showing them to her, he took the spare chair and sat down facing her.

"This house was built by a San Francisco shipping tycoon in 1910. It was a wedding gift for his second wife, whom he married shortly after the death of his first wife. Apparently, the first time he married for money and connections, and the second time he married for love. Local legend says they were very happy together, as were the next three couples who owned the place. The Millers were the last. Mr. and Mrs. Miller lived here for fifty wonderful years until they died within a few days of each other. Eventually their heirs decided to sell the house. There have been several interested parties, but no one has been serious about buying it until you.''

Rose raised her pale eyebrows. A slight smile teased at the corners of her full lips. "So if I buy the house, I'm joining a long line of happy marriages?"

"Something like that."

"I guess I need to start dating," she teased.

"Absolutely. It doesn't pay to mess with a legend."

A legend that explained why he and Josie hadn't bought the place. By the time they could afford to purchase the Miller place, their marriage had been in trouble. There were many things they had, but "being in love" wasn't one of them.

"I have great respect for tradition," she said, then sighed. "I must remember to put 'get married' on my to-do list."

He chuckled even as he tried to ignore the sense of relief at finding out there wasn't a husband in the picture. Not that it would make any difference to him. He didn't get involved with clients. Besides, he was seeing someone. Sort of. Actually the relationship was going nowhere. Jasmine was a nice woman but she was too young. They'd reached the awkward stage where she wanted to talk commitment and he wanted to move on.

"But I'll wait until Mr. Right comes along," she

said, leaning toward the table. "Tell me about your plans for my house."

He shifted his chair closer to hers and pointed to a drawing of the front elevation of the house. "I think it's important to maintain the integrity of the original design. The house was built by master craftsmen brought in from all over the country. The stair banister itself is a work of art. There are carved moldings, hand-fitted wood floors, and three exquisite chandeliers. My goal would be to work with everything that can be salvaged and saved, while making the house more modern and convenient."

She gazed at him while he spoke, her expression intent, as if she hung on every word. "Would you be deeply offended if I said I wanted to remodel the kitchen and bathrooms?"

"Not at all." He flipped through his papers and put a kitchen design on top. "That's completely possible while working within the existing measurements of the room."

He leaned toward the page. "I would suggest ripping out all the existing cabinets. They've been replaced twice before, so they have no connection with the original construction. I can make custom cabinets myself, combining a slightly old-fashioned design to match the feel of the house, while giving you modern conveniences such as pull-outs, granite countertops and new appliances."

"Sounds terrific."

A faint, sweet, floral scent drifted to him. He inhaled sharply, savoring the feminine fragrance. He wasn't much of a perfume kind of guy, but like everything else about her, this suited Rose. A knot of tension formed low in his belly—that had nothing to do with his desire to get the job and everything to do with his need to get to know this woman better. He wanted to slip his fingers through her sleek blond hair and feel it slide against his skin like cool silk. He wanted to taste her and touch her and—

He resurfaced to find her staring at him expectantly.

"What?" he asked, knowing he sounded like an idiot. "I mean, sorry. What were you saying?"

"I asked about plumbing and electrical. Will fixing them break the bank?"

"Ah, no. Not at all. Both have been completely redone in the past twenty years."

"Good."

She tapped a finger on the plan of the second floor. Her nails were oval and painted a light pink. Josie had never painted her nails. She hadn't had time. Between her job as a PE teacher, her exercise program and her coaching, she'd been on the run literally and figuratively. She had considered things like long hair, makeup and nail polish a waste of time. When he'd asked her to make time on special occasions, she'd rolled her eyes and told him if makeup was so darned important to him, he could wear it himself. She was what she was. Why did he want to make her over?

He hadn't been able to answer that before, and he still couldn't. He didn't expect a woman to be perfectly groomed at every moment of the day, but he also enjoyed knowing that she'd taken a little extra time for him.

"Now about this second floor."

Rose stared at the plans. There were three bedrooms and two baths. One of the bedrooms was larger than the other—obviously the old master suite.

She looked at him. "Why do the rooms seem smaller upstairs?"

"Because of the balcony." He showed her the front elevation again and pointed out the balcony encircling the entire second floor. "It looks terrific from the outside, but it eats up square footage." He hesitated, not sure he should butt in, but she *had* agreed to look at his plans. "There is a solution. The attic."

Rose glanced back at the front elevation, then ran her finger along the windows on the third floor. "What's there now?"

"Nothing. But it's plenty big." He flipped through pages and set the one he wanted on top. "I had this drawn up about four years ago."

"Why?"

It took him a second to figure out what she meant. Why did he have plans for a house he'd never owned? "At one time I thought of buying this place, but it didn't work out.

"Any regrets...about not owning the house?"

"Not even one," he said honestly. He and Josie would have killed each other during the remodeling. "This design turns the third floor into a master suite with a sitting area and another smaller bedroom." He shrugged. "It could be used for an office or a nursery for the baby's first couple of years. Until he was old enough to go to the second floor."

Rose nodded. "It could be a girl."

"Excuse me?"

"You said until 'he' was old enough to go to the second floor. I'm assuming a female child would get the same treatment. Or would you make her sleep out back with the dog?"

"No. Of course not. Any child. Or you could use the room for something else."

"No. I like the idea of a baby."

She looked at him as she spoke, her expression serious. But he saw the humor twinkling in her deep blue eyes. She liked the idea of a baby. Josie never had. They'd fought about that the last time they'd come to see this old house. He'd wanted to turn the third floor into the master suite. She'd wanted to use it as an exercise room. Kids hadn't been a part of her plan. They'd—

He rose to his feet so quickly, the chair tipped back and slammed into the floor. Del barely noticed. He rubbed his forehead, as if he could erase thought of his ex-wife from his mind. Why was he thinking about her so much? Damn. She'd been gone nearly three years, and he was happier without her. He wouldn't want her back on a bet. So why was she suddenly haunting him?

"Are you all right?"

He turned and saw Rose had pushed herself to her feet. She leaned on her cane. Concern pulled at the corners of her mouth. She looked like an angel standing there. Blond and beautiful. He supposed with her having a cane, some people might think she was also broken, but not him. She looked delightfully approachable and human. He'd had physical perfection once and it came at too high a price.

"I'm fine," he told her, forcing all thoughts of Josie out of his brain. He swore he wouldn't think about her again. His ex was gone and Rose was right here— apparently single. A good-looking, personable woman who liked old houses and wanted kids. Talk about perfect.

"Let me show you the kitchen," he said, crossing to the open area that housed painted cabinets and avocado-colored appliances. "We'd rip out everything and start from the bare walls."

He moved as he spoke, using his arms and hands to paint word pictures of wood cabinets, a double oven with a microwave and a center island cooktop. There was room for a pantry and even a desk work area.

"I like the window," she said, moving over to stand next to him. The greenhouse window had been added somewhere along the way, but it suited the graciousness of the house. "I'd like to grow fresh herbs and pretty flowers. I adore flowers."

He pictured her standing in a field full of wildflowers, which was crazy. Equally insane was the heat he felt in his blood. Blood that was thickening and moving distinctly south. If he didn't watch it, he was going to end up with a physical manifestation of his wayward thoughts. Not the polite thing when bidding on a remodeling job.

"The bathrooms upstairs will have to be redone, too, won't they?" she asked.

"They're about as ugly as the kitchen. The guest bath has dark and light pink tile."

She laughed. "Sounds attractive but not worth climbing a flight of stairs to see." She moved back to the table and touched the design for the third-floor master suite. "I want you to do this for me. All of it."

He stared at her. Just like that? "Don't you want an estimate?"

She tilted her head in a way that was so familiar, he had to take a step away from her. What was going on? He had the oddest sensation of being caught in both past and present.

"I heard you were honest, Del. Isn't that true?"

"Sure, but you don't want to take my word for it."

"Why not? I've heard you're good and that your prices are fair. So you're the one that I want. When can your crew start?"

He did some quick calculations. "I had a big job postponed, so next Monday. Does that work for you?"

"Absolutely. However I do have a request."

"Name it."

"I'd like the guest bath and one of the guest bedrooms to be done first and finished as quickly as possible. I'm living in a hotel and I don't want to stay there any longer than necessary. I'd prefer to be settled. If I won't be in the way, then the remodeling won't bother me at all."

Involuntarily his gaze drifted to her legs, hidden by the skirt of her dress. She hadn't wanted to climb the stairs today. Would next week be any different? But he didn't ask. Because it wasn't his business and he didn't want to embarrass her.

"I could have those two rooms ready by the end of the week. I'll put standard cabinets in the bathroom for now and replace them with custom later, when the third floor is done."

"Good idea. Escrow will close in ten days. I have their permission to go ahead with the remodeling, probably because I'm paying cash for the house and they already have all my money."

She smiled as she spoke. A feminine smile that hinted at a shared joke. He felt as if he'd taken an unexpected hit to the gut. All his air rushed out, but

that was the least of it. Even more powerful than the
need to breathe was the need to haul her close and
kiss her. He knew if he didn't taste her mouth and
feel her curvy body against his he would just up and
die. Simple as that.

The urge, the desire that had plagued him since
he'd arrived a half hour before, bothered him. Women
were a welcome part of his life, but they didn't usually take over. He wanted to ask Rose to tell him
every detail of her past. He wanted to find any other
man who had dared to touch her and beat the crap
out of him. He wanted—

He was crazy, he told himself. She was a client.
They weren't going to have a close and personal relationship. Besides, he'd already had one based on
mutual physical attraction. That had gotten him married and then divorced. He didn't plan to repeat either
experience. He didn't object to long-term relationships as long as they were grounded in compatibility
and complementing personalities...not his gonads.
Unfortunately, his body wasn't listening to logic just
now.

He forced his attention back to the job. "I'll have
to pull permits for the upstairs remodel," he said.
"I'll work on the paperwork and get it all filed when
escrow closes. In the meantime I'll have the office
draw up a contract along with an estimate of the work.
Where should I have the papers delivered?"

She named a local hotel.

"Does someone else need to look at any of this?"
he asked.

"Like my dad?"

"No. But a significant other, a lawyer?"

"Ah. Actually, I'm making this decision all on my own."

He was more pleased than he had a right to be. Figuring that his attempts for control were already shot, he gathered his papers and stuffed them back in his briefcase, then headed for the front door. She followed, walking more slowly. When he remembered the cane and her halting step, he slowed his so she could catch up. She opened the front door.

"I'm looking forward to this, Del."

"Me, too."

They shook hands. He ignored the way the feel of her skin against his made him want to rub his palm over all of her. He was disgusting. Worse, he was acting like a teenager. She waved, then closed the door behind him.

As he started down the path, he paused to glance over his shoulder and study the old house. At one time he'd imagined himself living here. Now there was going to be a different owner. He probed his heart and found that he didn't mind as much as he would have thought. To be honest, he couldn't imagine Josie and himself living together. His feelings for her were well and truly dead. Which meant he had to stop thinking about her and instead focus on the very appealing Rose. Hardly a difficult job. In fact, he was looking forward to spending a lot of time with her.

Two days later Josie sat in her hotel room studying the contracts Del's office had sent over. She read through the estimate of charges and a schedule of what would be completed when. Her pen hovered over the line for her signature.

Jan, from his office, had called to get her last name

for the contract and Josie had been forced to come up with a fake one. Which was the name she was expected to sign on the contracts. There were probably dozens of legal implications to her lie, she thought glumly. Not that she intended to run out on the bill. It would probably be easier for everyone if she just came clean and told Del who she was. Except she didn't want to.

Their conversation at the Miller place had been the first pleasant one she could remember. They'd been able to talk to each other like normal people, without screaming or accusing or either walking away. She'd found herself liking Del and enjoying teasing him. She'd liked the freedom of starting over as someone new. As Rose she could explore her relationship with Del from a safe distance, getting to know him again, finding out what she liked and didn't like. He was still too good-looking, with an amazing body. She'd always thought he was sexy, and that hadn't changed. But what did he think about her?

Josie leaned back in the club chair in her suite and sighed. She'd seen the spark of interest in Del's eyes. She knew her ex-husband well enough to know that he'd been attracted to the woman he thought of as Rose. After setting the contract on her lap, she pressed her fingertips to her face. She looked so different, but she thought her new face was pretty—albeit in a different way from her old one. She wasn't surprised that Del appreciated the more prominent cheekbones and smooth skin. He'd always liked her eyes and probably still did. So that interest made sense. What she didn't understand was how he could find anything appealing about her body.

She pressed her hands to her legs, feeling the tired

muscles quiver slightly. She was broken—nothing like she'd been before. How could he not be repelled by her weakness, her need for a cane? And yet he hadn't been. He'd been friendly, solicitous and charming. With completely twisted logic, she liked that he found her attractive, despite her disability, and she hated that he was over her enough to be interested in other women. Even if that woman was her.

She wasn't over *him*. Just spending an hour or so in his presence had been enough to convince her of that. She hadn't dated much since the divorce, telling herself she was busy figuring out her new life. But now she thought the truth might be very different. She'd never given herself the time or space to recover from losing Del. Instead she'd put her feelings in a box and ignored them. Being around him every day during the remodeling was going to force her into coming to terms with her past. She didn't look forward to the process, but she knew she would be stronger for having endured it.

Like physical therapy, her emotional recovery would be slow and painful, with plenty of setbacks. But it was the only way to be free of the man who used to be her husband.

Chapter Three

"I have the permits ready to go," Del told her from his seat behind his desk. "As soon as escrow closes I'll take care of it."

It was Monday morning and Josie had just spent a long weekend alone with way too much time to think. One of the things that had been on her mind was the reality that the name she'd given Del didn't match the name on the escrow papers. She'd never been a good liar and she still wasn't. Too much energy was required to keep everything straight. But she was in too deep now and she wasn't about to back out by telling Del the truth.

"Actually I've spoken with the escrow people," she said, forcing herself to stare into his dark eyes and pretend that everything was completely normal. "When I explained what I was doing, they offered to file the papers when they change the title. I'm heading over there this morning. I can take them with me.''

''Sounds like a plan,'' he said easily, as if nothing was wrong. Of course, for him nothing was.

''Good.'' She opened the oversize envelope on her lap and drew out the signed contracts. She set them on his desk, along with a cashier's check for one-third of the total amount required for the remodeling. ''I signed them and initialed the changes.''

''I like an efficient woman,'' he said, flashing her a smile.

She steeled herself against the crinkles by his eyes and the way his white teeth contrasted with his tanned skin. To distract herself from the overpowering maleness that was Delaney Scott, she looked around at his office.

He'd moved into a larger room since their divorce. Probably when his dad officially retired, she thought. The view was better—a big window overlooked the street. His old office had been in the back, next to the parking lot. As in the reception area, photos of restorations covered the walls. The cabinets and drafting table looked new, but the old wood desk was the same one he'd had for years. She recognized the gouge in the left-front corner—the result of a dropped circular saw. She knew that the middle drawer stuck, that he kept a stash of red licorice in the bottom drawer and that they'd made love on the desk at least a half dozen times. The last had been on a Sunday morning when he'd come into work to escape their latest fight, and she'd followed him, determined to have the last word. They'd been screaming at each other when the atmosphere had suddenly changed. One second they'd been saying how much they hated each other and the next they'd been tearing at clothes and kissing frantically.

Josie shifted uncomfortably as she tried to push the memory away. She wasn't sure which bothered her more—the wild-animal sex that required a flexibility she no longer had or the ugly things she and Del had said to each other.

"I've gone over the plans," Del was saying, drawing her attention to the present. "There shouldn't be a problem with getting an upstairs bedroom and the guest bath ready by Friday."

"I appreciate that. I don't like living in hotels."

He raised his eyebrows. "Let me see. Maids clean the room and make the bed, and room service delivers meals. What's not to like?"

"I guess when you put it that way, it doesn't make sense. But personally, I'd rather be in my own house."

What she didn't tell him was that having someone deliver meals and change her bed was too much of a reminder of all her months in the hospital and rehab center. She would rather be on her own and responsible for herself any day.

Del leaned back in his old leather chair. It creaked with the movement. He wore worn jeans and an old blue work shirt, both faded nearly white with age. The soft fabric molded to his body in a way that made her mouth water. Ironically, while she couldn't remember the last time she'd been with a man, she could remember the last time she and Del had made love. For once they hadn't been angry. Instead they'd both been sad—as if they'd known their relationship was ending.

"What about paint?" Del said. "You're going to

have to pick colors for the whole house eventually, but first I'll need suggestions for the bedroom and bath you want done this week. Also if you're interested in wallpaper, I have a couple dozen sample books you can look through. It's generally easier to take them home and look at them leisurely.''

She hadn't thought through all the details of remodeling a house. There were going to be a lot of decisions to make. ''Could we go neutral, say an off-white temporarily?''

''Not a problem.'' He made a note on a pad of paper.

She thought about wrestling all the wallpaper sample books from her car to the hotel room. It would take her hours to get them inside.

''As far as picking out wallpaper, what about bringing the sample books to the house? I'll be living there in a few days, anyway.''

''And checking up on me.'' His voice was teasing. ''Figures.''

''I'll admit I'm interested to see how it all comes together. It's difficult for me to look at a drawing and then imagine how the change is going to look in real life.''

He leaned forward. ''Spend as much time as you want watching. Seriously, Rose, this is going to be your home. You have every right to make sure you're getting exactly what you want. I hire skilled craftspeople who do excellent work. I have nothing to hide. In fact I would encourage you to check out the quality. I'm proud of my crew.''

''You also like what you do.''

He nodded. ''I'm lucky that way. I knew what I wanted from the time I was about eight and my dad started letting me tag along on jobs. For a while my folks tried to push me to become an architect, but I'd rather be building than drawing.''

There was an eagerness and excitement in his voice. She remembered all the times he'd wanted to talk about his work, and she'd told him that hearing about it was as interesting as watching paint dry. Had she been crazy? Del wasn't boring, he was a good, honest man. She sure had been a witch. The question was why? What had she been so angry about?

''I promise I won't get in the way,'' she said, forcing herself to relax and even smile. ''At least I'll try not to. I don't move all that quickly.''

Questions darkened his eyes, but he was too polite to ask. Josie found herself torn between wanting to share the details of her accident and knowing that it was too soon for those confessions. They might lead to others she wasn't ready to deal with. But she had a strong urge to tell him that she'd hadn't always been so broken. That there had been a time when she could walk and run just like a normal person.

Instead she rose to her feet and steadied herself with her cane. ''I'll leave you to get started, then,'' she said.

He stood and came around to her side of the desk. ''I'm looking forward to the project. Call me if you have any questions.''

Instead of offering to shake her hand, he lightly touched her arm. She felt the brush of his fingers and the resulting heat all the way down to the soles of her feet. It was as if he'd set fire to her blood. Talk about a complication. Being attracted to her ex-husband was a huge mistake.

She wanted to tell him that she was sorry she'd

been so difficult. After only a couple of conversations with Del, she'd remembered enough of the past to realize why they were divorced. It was one of the reasons she avoided dealing with the breakup. She hadn't wanted to know how much of the fault was hers. She didn't have a choice anymore. She was back where it had all started and she was here to get answers. Apparently from herself as well as Del.

She gave him a quick smile and hurried from the room, which for her meant an awkward hobble. Once in the safety of her car, she vowed that she would figure out what she needed from Del and tell him the truth as soon as possible. Just not today.

Wednesday morning she arrived at the house only to find the driveway filled with construction trucks. The familiar blue vehicles with the Scott Construction sign painted on the doors made her hesitate before climbing out of her Volvo. She'd been gone for three years, but most of Del's crew had worked for him much longer than that. Which meant she would know a good number of them. Del hadn't recognized her. Would they?

Josie thought about running away but knew she would have to face them all eventually. After all, by the end of the week she would be living in the house. She consoled herself with the fact that if her husband hadn't recognized her, no one else would, either. It wasn't much comfort but it was the best she could come up with under the circumstances. She sucked in a deep breath for courage, then began the laborious process of walking up to the front door and entering the Victorian mansion.

The sound of conversation and power tools filled

the old place. She stood just inside the foyer and breathed in the scent of wood, dust and change. Above her the old chandelier glittered in the bright morning light, while rays of sunshine illuminated floating clouds of dust.

Huge, heavy squares of canvas protected the hardwood floors from footsteps and spills. There were ladders leaning against walls, piles of tools and supplies in various corners and plans pinned up on walls. As she walked into the main room she saw a ratty old brown sofa and three recliners. She recognized the threadbare pieces of furniture. The crew carried them from job to job and sprawled on them during breaks, lunches and meetings.

Josie turned in a slow circle taking in the differences brought by only two days of work. Already the kitchen was gutted. Someone had chipped the tiles out of the guest bath on the first floor and a breeze cut through the house from an opening left by a removed window.

A tall, lanky man with bright-red hair walked by. He balanced several boards on one of his broad shoulders.

"Ma'am," he said, giving her a polite nod as he passed.

She smiled and reminded herself that calling Jerry or any of the men by name would be a mistake. She couldn't know them until they were introduced.

She followed his progress, noting that he didn't break stride or turn for a second look. She was a stranger to him. Which was good. She hadn't come this far to have her cover blown. She consoled herself with the thought that if this was a year ago, when she was still wrapped in bandages and could have easily doubled for a mummy woman, she would have sent the entire crew screaming for sanctuary.

"What's so funny?"

She hadn't realized she'd been smiling until she felt her lips straighten. She glanced up and saw Del standing in the entrance to the kitchen. He leaned against the door frame, looking as strong and handsome as ever, darn the man. Today he wore a navy T-shirt tucked into jeans. The soft fabric of the T-shirt clung to his chest, outlining every inch of muscle. Just to make her situation worse, she knew what he would look like without his clothes and that image was even better.

Her breath caught in her throat when he pushed off the support and walked toward her. Or maybe her breathing problem came from the fact that he actually sauntered. A slow, male movement that reminded her of a tiger staking out territory. Is that what he was doing with her? She desperately wanted to believe it was true.

"You were chuckling about something," he said when he came to a halt less than a foot in front of her. "Are you afraid we'll never get your house back together?"

"Not at all. I was thinking about some surgery I had a while back. How I would have frightened everyone if I'd come in wrapped in bandages."

"I think we would have survived."

He touched a hand to the small of her back, urging her to take a step to the side. As she did, a man of medium height but built like a fullback came through carrying armfuls of tools. She recognized Mark right away, but again didn't say anything to the man. Like Jerry, Mark gave her a polite nod.

She saw his gaze slide to the cane and then to her legs. Self-consciousness flooded her. Today was one of her bad days, when getting out of bed and forcing herself to stand had taken nearly all her reserves. She was stiff and suffering from muscle cramps and fatigue. The result of missing too many therapy sessions. But that couldn't be helped. Once she got settled in the house on Friday, she would find a therapist close by and get back to her treatments. Until then she would survive—on sheer will if necessary.

"Come see what we've done," Del said, pointing to the kitchen. "It's empty."

"I noticed. I guess I'm going to learn the phone number of every nearby takeout place, huh?"

He pointed to a list on the wall by a battered black phone. "Already done. Just part of the excellent Scott family service. I recommend the Chinese place. It's the best. So's the Mexican, but that's better at the restaurant because they have terrific margaritas."

He stepped back and touched a small refrigerator tucked under a makeshift counter made of sawhorses topped by plywood. "It won't hold a week's worth of shopping but it will get you by for now."

She pointed at a microwave sitting on top of the counter. "A loaner?"

"Exactly. We want you to be comfortable during the construction. Dust and noise can't be avoided but we try to make everything else as pleasant as possible." He slapped one hand against a bare wall. "As you can see the old cabinets are down. I've already taken measurements for the new ones and I'll get started on them this week. In the parlor you'll find an assortment of paint samples and wallpaper sample books for you to peruse in your free time. And in the main room you probably noticed our luxurious seating accommodations.''

She glanced over her shoulder at the ratty sofa. ''I thought that was the trash pile,'' she teased.

He stepped back, obviously outraged. ''It's an antique.''

''Uh-huh. Del, it's junk. I can see through patches of the fabric and there are springs poking out all over.''

''Having it around is kind of a tradition. Is it too offensive?''

''Not as long as it leaves when the job is over.''

''Deal. We have clean sheets we toss over the sofa and the recliners at the end of the day. So you'll have something clean to sit on.'' He paused and frowned. ''I never thought to ask. How much furniture are you going to be moving in?''

''Less than you'd think. I have a bedroom set being delivered Friday morning. Otherwise, just what I can fit in my car.''

''You travel light.''

''I've learned to.''

She'd spent the past year in three different hospitals and multiple rehab centers. Furniture hadn't been much of a priority. She still had a few things in the Los Angeles apartment she'd shared with her stepsister, Dallas, but saw no need to tell that to Del. Besides, she wasn't sure if she would be moving anything up to Beachside Bay. That sort of depended on whether or not she decided to stay here.

She remembered the contents of her car trunk. ''Did you already get paint for the guest bedroom and bath?'' she asked.

''No. Why?''

"I did some shopping this weekend and ended up buying paint and wallpaper."

His dark eyes brightened with laughter. "Let me guess. Pink and lavender. And the wallpaper had flowers on it."

"How very sexist."

"Am I wrong?"

She reached in her skirt pocket for her car keys. "Why don't you see for yourself. Everything is in the trunk."

He grabbed the keys, then called for one of the guys to get the supplies. "Want to show me what goes where?" he asked.

Del led the way to the stairs and waited for Rose to follow. She hesitated a moment before nodding her head in agreement and coming after him. He watched her walk, noticing that her movements were slower than usual, as if every step caused her pain.

"You all right?" he asked.

"Sure. Some days are easier than others. Today's turning out to be one of the hard ones."

As she spoke, he noticed the lines of tension and hurt around her eyes and mouth. She'd pulled her long blond hair back into a sleek ponytail that left her slender neck bare. A white T-shirt hugged her top half while a crinkly white and teal skirt fell to mid calf. He tried to concentrate on anything but the full curves outlined by her shirt. She was big enough to fill a man's hand and while he'd never considered himself much of a breast man, Rose made him rethink his position.

She started up the stairs. Her movements were slow and awkward, with her taking each step individually. She raised her right foot and set it firmly on the next level. The cane followed. She then braced herself on the cane and raised her left foot. He didn't know if she was in pain from what she was doing, but it sure hurt him to watch. He had to force himself not to hover behind her.

"Were you in an accident of some kind?" he asked before he could stop himself.

"Yes. A truck hit my car."

She spoke between sharp gasps of breath.

Del told himself not to watch, that if he had a brain in his head he would talk about something unrelated so that she wouldn't know he was itching to help in some way. Except she hadn't asked for help and he didn't know how to offer. But before he could think of a single thing to say, her left leg gave way and she started to go down.

She was less than a quarter of the way up the staircase. He was at her side, grabbing her arm and holding her upright before she even came close to falling. He wrapped one arm around her waist so she could lean on him.

They were close enough for him to inhale her floral scented perfume...and something else. Some female essence that was both attractive and oddly familiar. But before he could place it, she turned to look at him.

All thoughts fled his mind as he saw the pain and bleakness in her eyes. The blue irises darkened with a thousand emotions he couldn't begin to identify. He had no idea what she was going through or what she'd endured. He only knew that she didn't utter a word of complaint.

She trembled slightly, making him aware of their close proximity. His thumb was just under the curve of her right breast, and he was six kinds of an idiot for noticing. He also ignored the fact that her curvy rear rested against his thigh. All men were slime, he told himself, and he was the slime king.

"Do me a favor," he said as he bent down and slid his arm under her knees. "Don't scream too loud. You can yell at me when we get to the second floor."

Then he lifted her up into his arms and carried her the rest of the way up the stairs.

She fit him perfectly. Not like Josie, who had been bony and too muscular. Rose was soft curves and yielding femininity. He wanted to keep on walking with her like this, taking them both to a quiet spot where they could get to know each other better. He wanted to bend down and kiss her until…hell, he didn't want to *stop* kissing her.

Unfortunately, neither was an option so when they reached the landing, he set her on her feet and prepared to be castigated.

"I know," he said, holding up a hand to try to slow her down. "I violated every code in the cane users handbook. I shouldn't have picked you up and carried you. If you'd wanted my help you would have asked. I'm insensitive and a jerk. I just couldn't stand to watch you in pain and I was afraid you'd fall. For all I know you'd break your neck and die right here and I know you haven't had time to put the house into your will. What if your estate defaulted on the contract? So it was really about money. I wasn't trying to insult you."

Her mouth twitched up slightly at the corners. "Well, if you were just being mercenary and looking out for your self-interest, I guess I understand. But if you were trying to be nice, I'd have to be mad."

She was laughing at him. "Are you mad?"

"That you were nice and caring and a gentleman? Not at all. Just don't tell me I need to lose a few pounds."

He allowed himself to give her body the once-over, lingering a tiny bit on her breasts. "From here you look great."

She laughed, although the sound had a slightly strangled quality. "Thank you. For the compliment and for carrying me. I don't think we should make a habit of it, but under the circumstances, it was very nice."

He almost added "for me, too" but caught himself at the last minute.

"I do have a question, though," she said in her low, husky voice. The sound definitely rubbed him the right way. He could listen to her for hours.

"Shoot."

"Would you have done it if I'd been a man?"

It took him a second to realize what she meant. Would he have carried her up the stairs if she'd been male? He hesitated, knowing the right answer and not sure he could actually say it.

"Politically correct battles with gut truth." She leaned close. "Don't try to pretend otherwise. I can see it in your eyes."

"Yeah, yeah, so I wouldn't have carried a guy up the stairs. I still would have helped."

"Hey, boss. Where do you want these?"

Gary came up the stairs with a perfectly timed interruption. He held a couple of cans of paint in each hand and had rolls of wallpaper tucked under his left arm.

"Just leave them here," Del said, pointing to a

corner of the landing. "The rooms aren't ready for them yet."

Gary deposited the supplies and left.

Del crouched to check the colors of the cans. The paint was a sunny shade of yellow. There was a border print of ivory tea roses accented in green. A matching pattern of smaller flowers filled the full-size wallpaper rolls.

"Just what I thought," he muttered. "Girl stuff."

"These rooms *are* for me," Rose said lightly. "What did you expect? Monster trucks or half-naked women?"

"I've never seen half-naked-woman wallpaper, but it's a thought."

"Yes, especially if they're young, perfect women."

"It's a plus, but not necessary."

As he spoke he wondered if she felt she wasn't perfect anymore. Yeah, she used a cane and probably had some scars, but that didn't really matter. At least not to him. Had some male moron hurt her by making her feel she wasn't enough?

He didn't know how to ask and it wasn't his business, so instead he stood and motioned to the guest bathroom.

"Want to check out what we've done so far?"

"Sure." She turned and led the way. "I'm guessing it's gutted and not much else."

"You have to use your imagination."

He showed her that they were going to turn the tub/shower combination which would allow them to fit in a vanity with a double sink.

Rose nodded slowly, then looked at him. "But what about the toilet? Moving things around will be awkward to get in and out of the room."

"Not if we move the door hinge to the other side, so it opens to the left and not the right."

She studied the door and nodded. "Very clever. This would be one of the many reasons why I'm not trying to do this myself. I wouldn't have thought of that."

"It's why we get the big bucks. Now, in the bedroom itself we're replacing the window, doing some patching, then painting on Wednesday. That will give us forty-eight hours to clear out the paint smell."

"Which isn't going to happen."

"No, but it will be better than if we painted it Friday morning. The bathroom gets patched this afternoon, painted tomorrow. Tub, sink and toilet go in on Thursday."

"Which is a good thing. My alternative is to use the hose out back for a shower."

"While that would entertain the neighbors, it's still a little cool in the morning, so I wouldn't recommend it."

"Oh, gee, thanks. And here I'd been looking forward to some al fresco bathing."

He didn't want to think about that. Actually he did want to think about it in great detail, but that would be a big mistake. "Are you going to be all right here by yourself? It's a big house, and you're not even going to have a kitchen."

She leaned against the wall, bracing herself. He wondered if her leg was bothering her.

"I'm having a phone line run in tomorrow," she said. "That means I won't be cut off from the world. As for the kitchen, between the microwave and your list of takeout, I'll be fine."

"You don't cook?"

She hesitated. "Not much. I didn't used to at all, but I've been slowly teaching myself."

Josie didn't cook, either, but with her it was a matter of principle. They'd never gotten far enough past the fighting for him to know if she'd even known how. He shook his head as if to clear it. He didn't understand his sudden obsession with his ex-wife.

She looked at him and smiled. "I don't want to keep you, Del. Thanks for the tour. I'll let you get back to work."

The problem was he didn't want to be anywhere but with her. In fact, he could think of several ways for them to spend the day together and only about half of them involved getting naked.

Instead he asked if she would be all right going down the stairs on her own.

"Down is much easier than up," she informed him.

With no brilliant excuse suddenly presenting itself, he found himself leaving, both her presence and the house. Because he had things to do at the office, then he had to start working on her kitchen cabinets. But he found himself thinking about her throughout the day. About the way she laughed and smelled and felt in his arms. And the way he'd wanted to kiss her more than he'd wanted anything in a real long time.

Chapter Four

Friday morning Josie sat curled up on the sheet-covered sofa in her new house. All around her the sound of construction and people made her feel that she was a part of something positive. She was probably in the way, but having to duck large sheets of lumber and listen to the whine of saws was far better than sitting alone in her hotel room. She'd hated the solitude and the impersonal decorations. Although she would still be by herself when she moved into this house, at least it would be *hers*. She could do what she liked in the way of decorating and make it a real home. Something she hadn't had in a year.

She returned her attention to the wallpaper sample book in her lap and flipped the page. Her eyes widened as she stared at a horrible print of huge bright-blue roses surrounded by gold and pink birds.

"As your contractor, I'm afraid I can't let you do that to any innocent room in this house."

At the sound of the familiar voice a shiver rippled up her spine. The hairs at the back of her neck stood and quivered and her heartbeat jumped into overdrive. She'd been back in Beachside Bay less than two weeks, and already she was acting like a teenager with her first crush around Del. Talk about trouble.

She glanced up and over her shoulder. Her ex-husband stood behind her, leaning forward, his hands braced on the back of the sofa. He pointed at the open wallpaper sample book.

"You're kidding right?" he said. "That one would win an ugly competition, no problem."

She studied the offending square of paper. "You don't like it? But the colors would give me so much to work with." She was careful to keep any sound of teasing out of her voice.

He looked at her. She was close enough to see the flecks of gold that brightened his dark irises and the lines fanning out from the corners of his eyes. Her gaze shifted so that she was staring at his mouth, remembering what it had felt like when they'd kissed all those years ago and making her wonder if it would be different now.

He straightened and came around to stand in front of her. He planted his hands on his narrow hips. "You can't be serious. Rose. Come on. I know I'm a guy and all my taste is in my mouth, but even I can see that's hideous."

She puffed out her lower lip in a slight pout. "Del, I hate to put you in your place, but you're the contractor, not the decorator. I really like this and I'm going to order it. I thought maybe for the parlor."

"No guy on the planet wants to live in a house with blue flowers on the wall."

"I know, but wouldn't cages of little white birds look charming against the blue and gold? And one of those all-white cats. The fluffy kind."

His gaze narrowed even as the corners of his mouth turned up. "Brat. You're teasing me."

She held up the book. "You deserved it. I can't believe you'd think anyone sane would buy this wallpaper."

"Hey, they put it in the sample book for a reason. Not only is it available to order, but people have."

"I hadn't thought of that." She studied the print more closely and shuddered. "Of course there is good news should I go ahead and buy this."

"Do enlighten me."

She grinned. "According to you, no man on the planet would want to live in a house with this on a wall. So I do one room in it and when I have a horrible date I want to get rid of, I simply put him in there and he'll run screaming from my life."

"You need a different plan," he said, settling next to her on the sofa and taking the book from her lap. "If the guy's that awful, you don't invite him home."

"I suppose you're right."

He looked at her. "How long has it been since you were on a date?"

His question made her feel self-conscious. She smoothed the skirt of her dress and cleared her throat. "Yes, well, after the accident, my social life wasn't as full as it had been before." Which was *almost* true. She'd barely dated anyone since her divorce. The accident had forced her to go from a couple of dates a year to none. Not a huge difference. But Del didn't have to know that. "There was the male nurse who brought me ice cream that one time, but I don't think that counts."

He returned his attention to the sample book and began flipping pages. "Then you're going to need a refresher course. Rule number one—no strangers in the house. Get to know the guy before you invite him over."

"Yes, sir," she said, figuring there was no point in telling him that the odds of her dating anytime soon were unlikely. For one thing, she was back in town because she wanted closure with Del—not because she was looking to get involved. Second, she couldn't imagine a man being interested in her and asking her out. Not with her cane, her limp and her scars.

"What about this one?"

He pointed at a sample of ivory paper with a half-inch wide gold stripe bracketed by a burgundy pin-stripe. The paper was elegant and very attractive. Josie looked at him in surprise.

"That's nice."

"You sound shocked."

"Of course. You said all your taste was in your mouth."

He surprised her even more by lightly touching her cheek.

"I lied," he said, handing her the book and getting to his feet. "I have pretty good taste. Some of it is innate, some I learned from my mom and my ex-wife. But before you go wild on wallpaper, we need to talk about paint."

He crossed to the far side of the room and picked up several wide rings holding dozens of paint samples. Josie was vaguely aware of the fit of his jeans, but she was also conscious of the fact that this was the first time he'd mentioned being married before. She wanted to stop him and ask him what he thought of her…of his ex-wife. Did he remember their time together with anything but annoyance? Did he have regrets, like she did?

But before she could form the question, he was back at her side, handing her several paint samples. "My suggestion is that you take advantage of the rooms that have afternoon light. Go for the warmer tones, because the sunlight has a golden cast in the afternoon. Especially during the summer. Something about being by the beach. I don't know the physical reasons for it, but I know it exists."

"I appreciate the input."

They flipped through the samples together and picked out colors for the dining room and kitchen. Del was knowledgeable and easy to get along with. He made suggestions but didn't push. Josie was surprised. What she remembered about him was that he was determined to have his way and she was just as determined to be the victor. What had changed? Had each of them grown up in their time apart or was it just her? Had she simply assumed Del wanted his way and reacted accordingly without bothering to find out the truth?

There was no way to get an answer to that question. Not without having a conversation she wasn't ready for. Confessing the truth about herself was something she was going to have to do pretty soon, although she knew she would put it off as long as reasonably possible. She liked her new relationship with Del. It was fun and easy. He liked her. When they were married he hadn't liked her much at all.

A knock on the open front door caught their attention. Del rose and walked over to greet two men standing in the foyer. One held a clipboard.

"We're here to deliver some furniture."

"My bedroom set," Josie said.

Del nodded. "This is the place. Let me show you where it goes."

He and the man with the clipboard climbed the stairs. The day before, Josie and Del had discussed the layout of her new bedroom. The room had been patched and painted. There was a new window in place, complete with a window shade. She would worry about curtains later. The small guest bath was finished, as well. She leaned on her cane and slowly pushed herself to her feet so she was standing when Del came down the stairs a few minutes later.

"Looks like everything is going to fit," he said. "There's plenty of room. They'll put the furniture together and then you can go up and inspect their work."

"Maybe I should start climbing the stairs now so I can be at the top when they finish." She said the words matter-of-factly. She wasn't feeling sorry for herself, she was simply stating the truth.

"I think you can probably wait twenty minutes or so," he teased in reply. "Or I can carry you again." He gave her a quick wink. "I like carrying pretty young women upstairs. It makes me feel macho."

He was flirting with her. Josie didn't know what to make of that. She felt herself blushing, which was crazy. She never blushed. "I, um… Thanks, but I think I'll make it under my own steam, such as it is."

"If you're sure. But my services are available to you whenever you would like. Just say the word."

He leaned close to whisper in her ear. "It's the dresses. Too many women wear jeans. I'm a sucker for a woman in a soft kind of floaty dress, like you wear all the time. I can't resist."

His words made her start to melt inside. At the same time she felt a swift stab of pain. She'd never been a dress person before. Jeans and sweats had allowed her to move the way she liked. Or shorts. Before the accident she'd been more concerned with being active than being feminine.

"I'm glad you approve," she said shyly. "Probably reminds you of your mother."

As soon as the words fell out of her mouth, she wanted to call them back. Catherine Scott *was* the sort of woman who wore dresses rather than slacks. It had been just one of dozens of differences between the women.

Del frowned. "How'd you know?"

"Good guess. A lot of moms are like that."

She shrugged hoping he would accept her answer. She didn't want to get into a conversation about his mother. Catherine had been a devoted homemaker and a brilliant cook. A couple more places where Josie hadn't been able to measure up.

Del touched her arm. Just a light brush of his fingers, but against her bare skin it was highly erotic. She felt herself swaying toward him.

"I'll admit that my mom wears dresses, but despite that, you don't make me think of her at all. Just so we're clear on that."

"Okay." She shifted awkwardly, not sure if she should say anything else.

Male appreciation flashed in his eyes. Male appreciation and something she wanted to think was sexual interest. She was both thrilled and cautious. He couldn't be interested in her in that way, could he? Yes, they got along and conversation was easy between them, but being naked was something completely different. Besides, he was still supposed to be pining for, well, her.

"I've got to get back to work," he said. "Kitchen cabinets are calling to me. You have my pager number if you need to get in touch with me, right?"

She nodded.

He left and some of the light seemed to go out of the room. Josie returned to the sofa and slumped onto a lumpy cushion. She was playing a dangerous game. If Del was really starting to like her as Rose, he wasn't going to be happy to find out she'd been lying to him. Which meant she should probably tell him the truth as soon as possible. But she didn't want to. But she had to.

She sighed. All right. She'd do it the next time she saw him. No matter what, she would explain who she was and why she'd returned. He would understand…eventually. She would explain everything until things were all right between them again. And then they would decide what they each wanted from the other. Which meant that between now and then she had to figure that out for herself.

By five-thirty that afternoon, everyone was gone. Josie stood alone in the nearly empty house and listened to the silence. The sharp smell of paint blended with the homey scent of cut wood. She felt a little lost and lonely, but it was still better than being in a hotel—or worse, a hospital.

After the crew had left, she'd brought in her suitcases. She had four small ones, because they were more manageable for her than one large one. She'd already carried the first one up the stairs and would tackle the rest over the course of the evening. The remaining three were positioned neatly by the foot of the stairs.

Using her cane to assist her movements, she walked into the parlor that she was going to make into a living room and library. The chair rail had been removed from the two walls that would support the built-in bookshelves. White patches to repair cracks and nail holes contrasted with the light-green paint favored by the previous owner. Notations on the wall showed where the frame for the shelves would go. Del had explained they were being custom built at the company's main workshop and would be installed in pieces. Her kitchen cabinets would come in the same way.

From the foyer Josie made her way into the main family room. Several battered floor lamps stood around the perimeter of the room, each plugged into a socket. Del had volunteered their services after noticing she really didn't have any furniture of her own save the newly delivered and set-up bedroom set. He'd been worried as he left and had voiced his concern about her being here all by herself.

Josie sank onto the sheet-covered sofa. She wasn't sure how she felt about his concern. While she appreciated the attention, she'd always been completely self-sufficient. That had been one of the problems in their marriage. He'd wanted her to need him, and she hadn't wanted to need anyone.

The last year had taught her differently. She'd been forced to depend on everyone from medical personnel to her family, just to survive. There had been weeks when she hadn't been able to do a single thing for herself except breathe. In some ways the experience had broken her spirit, but in others it had made her stronger. Either way, she'd changed. She wasn't the woman Del had known three years ago. She didn't look the same, move the same or think the same.

Sometimes Josie felt as if she'd completely lost herself. At other times she knew she'd been given a precious gift.

As she looked around the bare room, the phone on the floor by the sofa caught her attention. She glanced at her watch, then picked up the instrument and set it on her lap.

Close to six on a Friday night. Most people would have already left for home. Most, but not all. She dialed a familiar number. The phone on the other end rang only once before being answered by a strong, no-nonsense voice.

"Fitzgerald."

"Hi, A.J., it's your better half."

There was a moment of silence followed by a chuckle. "Josie, I keep telling you. *I'm* the better half. You're the tagalong."

She smiled as she leaned back against the sofa and closed her eyes. Just hearing her twin brother's voice was enough to make her feel safe. The familiar teasing made her miss him.

"It's Friday night," she said. "Why aren't you out on the town with a bimbo on each arm?"

"Because I don't date bimbos."

"You don't date at all. You're worse than me. At least I used to be married, which is more than you can say. Tell me you're seeing someone."

"I have a beautiful, brown-eyed blonde in my life," he said easily.

"A.J., your dog doesn't count."

"She'll be crushed to know her aunt Josie is dismissing her so cruelly. But enough about me. What's going on in *your* life?"

"I'm not ready to change the subject." She opened her eyes and stared at the empty fireplace in front of her. "I'm serious, A.J. You work too hard, you don't have a social life. When do you take time for yourself?"

There was a moment of silence. Josie could picture her twin leaning back in his big leather chair and turning until he could see out across downtown Seattle. A.J. was a successful financial planner who handled sums of money she couldn't even imagine. He'd risen quickly through the ranks of his company and now had a corner office and a client list that would make any competitor drool. With the tall, blond Fitzgerald good looks and an intelligent, gentlemanly manner, he was pestered by women on a regular basis. But he rarely accepted their invitations.

"I'm in my career mode," A.J. said calmly. "When I'm where I want to be, I'll worry about a personal life."

"All the good ones will be taken."

"That's a possibility I'll deal with at the time. Now tell me about you. Dallas said you'd left L.A. Where are you?"

She hesitated before answering. He wasn't going to like what she had to say. "Beachside Bay."

There was a long pause from his end of the phone. "Digging up ghosts?"

"Something like that. I'm dealing with my past. It wasn't as behind me as I'd thought."

"Are you taking care of yourself physically? Your last surgery wasn't all that long ago."

"Tell me about it." Josie rubbed her left thigh. The ache there was her constant companion. "I'm doing okay."

"What does 'okay' mean? Are you doing your exercises and getting to physical therapy? Are you getting plenty of rest?"

"I've been...adjusting. Right now I need to heal my spirit before I worry about my body."

"That sounds like a line if you ask me," he grumbled. "What do you think Katie would have to say about it?"

Katie, their oldest sister, was a physical therapist. She would have plenty to say, none of it nice. She would order Josie back into physical therapy and probably threaten to fly out and take care of it herself.

"Katie's busy with our new niece. Serena is only eight weeks old."

"I suspect she'd make time for you, kid."

"I know, but it's not necessary."

She clutched the phone tightly and felt his worry, even from nearly a thousand miles away. Knowing that he cared made her feel warm inside. From the moment he'd found out about her accident, A.J. had been at her side. He'd stayed with her through the first few surgeries, then had visited her regularly over the past year. All her siblings had. Even David, who had a sick wife and four daughters.

"You have to take care of yourself, Josie," A.J. said gruffly.

"I know. And I am. I'll get back on track with the physical therapy. I promise."

"Good. I talked to Mom. She says everything is fine in Lone Star Canyon. They're expecting a good year on the ranch."

Josie pressed her lips together in annoyance. "I'm glad to hear it."

A.J. continued talking about the goings on at the Fitzgerald ranch, but she wasn't listening. She was caught up in the fact that he called their stepmother "Mom."

Josie sighed. Her father had married Suzanne seventeen years ago, and while the other children had accepted her easily, she and Josie had never gotten along. Josie wasn't sure why. Maybe because she'd never forgiven Suzanne for being alive when her real mother had died so unexpectedly.

"Did she say anything about Dad?" she asked.

"Just that he was healthy and as stubborn as ever." A.J. gave a short laugh. "You're not expecting to hear that he's changed are you?"

"No. Of course not."

But Josie was lying. She *did* want to hear that Aaron was different than he had been. That passing time had mellowed him into a gentler version of his very tough self. She dreamed about it because, of all the Fitzgerald children, she was the most like him. Watching his stubbornness, his unyielding determination, his willingness to alienate everyone he loved just to be right had always made her uncomfortable. Mostly because she had some of those same qualities in herself and she was desperately trying to change.

But as much as she might dislike parts of herself, she knew she owed her very survival to the stubborn-

ness inherited from her father. When she'd first been
injured and the doctors had outlined her long, seem-
ingly impossible road to recovery, she'd felt defeated
before she'd even begun. Aaron had been the one to
stand by her bed and remind her that she was a Fitzgerald and Fitzgeralds never quit. Not for a moment,
no matter how long it took or how much it hurt.

"Are you all right in Beachside Bay by yourself?"
A.J. asked.

She recognized the unspoken part of the question.
Are you all right being around Del?

"It's weird," she admitted. "But in a good way. I
want to get some things straight in my mind. Once
that's done I feel like I can then put the past behind
me and get on with my life."

"Good for you." He hesitated. "You know I'm
always here for you, kid, right?"

She smiled. "Yes. I know. And I love you, too,
A.J. Now shut off your computer and go do something fun. Promise?"

"I'll do my best. Talk to you soon.

"Okay. Bye."

She hung up the phone and sat alone in the silence.
But the quiet didn't seem quite so unfriendly now.
She knew that if she needed to talk to A.J. again, he
would make time for her, as would the rest of her
family. Especially Dallas.

The thought of her stepsister made her smile. Josie
and Suzanne might have had some troubles in their
relationship, but it hadn't been like that with Josie
and Dallas. They were three years apart in age, but
they'd always gotten along. When Josie had left Del,
Dallas had been looking for a roommate as she studied at UCLA. They'd gotten an apartment together,

and Josie had picked up the pieces of her life. The summer after the accident, Dallas had been her constant companion, seeing her through the first several surgeries. Like Aaron, Dallas had urged her to never give up.

And she hadn't. Because of her refusal to quit, she used a cane instead of a wheelchair. In time, with another surgery, she would be strong enough to walk on her own. She'd done what had to be done, regardless of the cost to her in pain and effort. She'd—

Josie sat up suddenly and blinked in the rapidly darkening room. She hadn't been a quitter after the accident, but what about before? She and Del had fought for a long time, but ultimately she'd been the one to walk away from the marriage. Why had she given up on the two of them?

She rubbed her temple as she thought about the past. She'd been so awful to Del—always pushing back, never compromising. She'd never cared about his work or wanted to talk about it. She'd never noticed what a good, kind man he was. Now, three years too late, she realized that she genuinely liked being around him. He made her laugh.

She shook her head in an effort to get him out of her brain. Thinking about him like that wasn't constructive. But as she turned, she caught sight of the stairs and couldn't help remembering him carrying her up them a few days before. She'd loved being so physically close to him. He'd been so familiar and she'd felt welcomed back. Her body had responded with a hunger that had shocked her. As if she'd been waiting for him all this time.

"Crazy," she murmured aloud. She and Del might be able to find a friendship out of the ashes of their past, but they couldn't be any more than that. A physical relationship was impossible. She was too different from how she'd been before. Too...wrong.

Her lack of physical activity had meant that she'd put on weight. She wasn't fat, but she sure wasn't as toned and lean as she had been. The entire shape of her body had changed. Plus there were all those scars.

Unable to stop herself—even though she knew it was a mistake—Josie rose and walked into the small powder room just off the foyer. The toilet and sink were missing, but there was still an oval mirror hanging on the dark-papered wall. She stared at herself, at the stranger's face looking back at her.

Her last facial surgery had been six months before. Nearly all the swelling was gone and the scars had faded as the doctor had promised. She looked completely normal, yet completely different. After twenty-seven years of being one person, now she was someone else. At least on the outside.

But what about on the inside? How much of her was the same and how much was different? The questions made her uncomfortable. She turned to leave and stumbled over a bit of uneven flooring. Without her cane she would have fallen. As it was, she could barely keep her balance.

Frustration filled her. There had been a time when she'd been able to run and jump and test her body. She'd moved with a natural grace she'd always taken for granted. She would never be that other woman again. That part of her had been destroyed in less than a heartbeat.

Pain filled her. Not the physical kind, but an ache of the soul. She wanted to turn back time. She wanted to be her old self. She wanted a normal body. She—

A knock on the door surprised her. She turned toward the sound, then began to walk in that direction. When she reached the foyer, she flipped on the porch light and opened the door. Del stood on her porch, looking slightly sheepish and holding out two bags labeled with the name of a local Chinese restaurant.

"If I'm interrupting a hot date, I'll leave," he said. "Otherwise, I thought you might like some company. And if you just want the food, that's fine, too."

Her sadness fled as if it had never been. She felt herself grinning at him. "My hot date passed out when I showed him my wallpaper selections. So I would welcome your company." She pushed the door open wider. "Come on in."

Chapter Five

Josie hoped that her extreme pleasure at seeing Del didn't show. If he knew how hard her heart was pounding and that she couldn't think of a single intelligent thing to say, he would wonder if she ever got out these days and if there was something wrong with her.

"I hope you like Chinese," he said as he walked into the main room, turning on lights as he went. "I decided on half orders of several different entrées so we'd have a choice."

"Sounds great. Chinese is one of my favorites."

She trailed after him, her uneven gait much slower than his. By the time she reached the sofa, he'd already pulled up the rickety folding table and set the bags on top of it. From one he pulled several small cartons of steaming food. The delicious smell made her mouth water and her stomach growl. From the other bag he drew out thick paper plates, plastic utensils and two bottles of beer.

He tapped the latter on their caps. "There's soda in the refrigerator if you'd prefer that."

She smiled. "No. Beer is great."

She and Del might have fought about nearly everything, but Chinese food dishes and imported beer hadn't ever been a problem. On that they'd agreed perfectly.

He motioned to the sheet-covered sofa. "If the lady would be so kind as to take a seat, the gentleman will serve the meal."

His elegant speech and deep bow were at odds with his red flannel shirt and worn jeans. Josie couldn't help a small smile of contentment as she settled on the sofa and set her cane on the floor. Del moved the table close, then unfastened the cap on the bottles and set one in front of her.

He'd thought of everything, even napkins and cheap wood chopsticks.

"I'm too hungry to mess with those," she said when he offered her a pair. "I'll use a fork, thank you very much."

"As the lady wishes." He opened the cartons and displayed their contents. "Egg rolls and paper wrapped chicken. Kung pao chicken, orange-flavored beef, sweet and sour pork, shrimp with lobster sauce, fried rice and steamed rice. What would you like?"

Everything looked tempting. Josie hesitated only a second before pointing to the orange-flavored beef and the shrimp with lobster sauce. "I'll start with those, along with steamed rice. But you don't have to serve me. I can do it."

"I'm showing off," he said, scooping the food

onto a paper plate. "You're responsible for your own seconds."

After he handed her a full plate, he sat next to her on the sofa and served himself. Then he held up his beer bottle. "To old houses and new friends."

She picked up her drink and clinked it against his. "Thanks, Del."

"You're welcome. Now eat."

She did as he requested, taking a sip of the beer before diving into the Chinese food. Her heart was still line dancing inside her chest, and her nerves felt a little quivery having him so close. She couldn't believe he'd stopped by with dinner. His kindness made her happy and apprehensive at the same time. She got the impression that he liked her. Except the woman he liked—Rose—wasn't who he thought. He was going to be angry when he found out the truth.

She should probably tell him now. Just blurt out the words. Except she didn't want to spoil a potentially lovely evening. She'd been so alone for so long. Was it terribly wrong to want to enjoy Del's company for a little while before she had to ruin everything between them?

She didn't have an answer, or if she did, she didn't want to think about it. So for now...for today at least...she would continue to keep her secret just a little longer.

"Do you like it?" he asked, pointing to her plate and the beer. "I thought you might be more of a wine woman, but I took a chance."

"Everything is wonderful." She nibbled on a shrimp and swallowed.

As she savored the delicate flavors she suddenly realized that the dishes he'd chosen had all been his favorites. Some of her humor faded as she remembered the times they'd argued about what to order. As she studied the open cartons she realized that she liked these items, too. There were a few other dishes that she would enjoy as much, but it wasn't as if she'd hated Del's favorites. But even in picking Chinese food, she'd insisted on being right. She hadn't been willing to take turns or have them each pick an entrée. Why had she been so difficult all the time?

"Do you eat here often?" she asked, pointing at the name on the bag.

He grinned. "About twice a week. I'm not much of a cook." He shrugged. "Now that I'm on my own, I wish I'd learned, but my mom never taught me."

"You could teach yourself."

"What? And be a responsible person? Naw. Takeout is better."

Humor glinted in his eyes. She took in the slightly damp hair and the clean line of his jaw. He'd obviously showered and shaved before dropping by with dinner. Josie told herself not to read too much into his actions. Maybe he was just being nice. But in her heart she wanted it to be more than that. She wanted Del to be attracted to her, while at the same time she feared his interest. Not only because of the lie she was living, but because she was so different from what she'd been before.

"I'm surprised your mother would send you out in the world so unprepared," she said.

"I guess she thought there would always be a woman around to take care of me. Plus I'm an only child. I was spoiled."

"Really?" She couldn't keep the surprise out of her voice.

"You're shocked that she would cater to me? A lot of moms do—especially if they only have one child."

"No. I'm surprised you'd admit it."

It was something she'd accused him of dozens of times when they'd been married. She told him that Catherine's catering to his needs had made it difficult for anyone else not to fall short of his expectations. At the time he'd told her she was paranoid.

He drank from his beer bottle. "My mom is one of those women who believe that taking care of her family is the most important thing in her life. She helped at the business, took care of the house, catered to my dad and me. If there was a burned piece of something or a smaller serving, she claimed it for herself. If there was a draft, she sat in it."

"She sounds like a saint," Josie said, careful to keep her voice neutral. Saint Catherine, she thought grimly. How many times had her mother-in-law's actions been thrown in her face? Although she'd liked Del's mother, she'd never come close to measuring up, and eventually she'd stopped trying. Her greatest goal had never been to be a servant in her own home.

"She was old-fashioned," Del admitted. "But she's changed."

Josie scooped some sweet and sour pork onto her plate. "What do you mean?"

"About two years ago my mom went on strike. She said she was tired of catering to my dad, of working part-time at the business and full-time at home. He got weekends off but she was expected to still cook and clean and take care of him. Who was taking care of her?"

"Your mother said that?" Josie blurted out before

she could stop herself. Saint Catherine had lost control?

"Absolutely. She and my dad fought about it for weeks. They nearly split up. She said she wanted a fifty-fifty relationship, and he wasn't willing to give up his personal maid. At least that's how she described it. My dad's version was a little different."

Josie blinked in surprise. She remembered all the times she and Catherine had talked about Del. His mother had always taken his side, telling Josie that she had to be the one to bend, the one to make Del feel special. Josie had wanted to know when her new husband was going to make *her* feel special, as well. She'd never thought Catherine had once heard a word she'd said, but maybe she'd been listening after all.

"What happened? Are they still together?"

"Oh, yeah. Dad couldn't live without her. She moved out for about forty-eight hours. She went to San Francisco and spent a couple of days at a luxury hotel. Apparently she had the time of her life. Some business guy even tried to pick up on her in the hotel restaurant. My dad fell apart. He begged her to come home and swore everything would be different."

"Is it?"

"Sure is. She told him she wanted him to retire and for them to spend more time together. They decided to buy a motor home, and now they spend most of the year driving across the country. They're having a great time, and my dad has learned to cook."

Who would have thought? She wanted to ask more questions about Catherine's transformation but didn't know how without giving herself away.

"So they left you in charge of the business," she said instead. "Do you like that?"

He shrugged. "It wasn't a big surprise. I'd been taking over more and more of the responsibility over the past few years. Business has been booming. Despite being out of the way, Beachside Bay is growing. We've had more work than we can handle, even with bringing on more employees."

He leaned forward and got another helping of food. "Enough about me," he said. "Where did you live before you came to Beachside Bay?"

Josie hesitated. She didn't know how much Del knew about his ex-wife's life. Not that he seemed to be linking Rose with Josie.

"I lived in Los Angeles. I was a teacher—at least until a year ago."

He set down his plate. "That's when you had the accident, right?"

She nodded. "That changed everything."

"Do you mind talking about it? I would like to know what happened, but not if it will bother you."

She didn't mind sharing the details of what had happened, but she was a little nervous about giving him too many clues to her real identity. She finished her last mouthful of food and put her plate on the table in front of them.

"I was driving home for lunch when a truck ran the red light and hit me broadside. The brakes had failed so it was going pretty fast when it slammed into me."

He shifted so that he was angled toward her. "That sounds ugly."

"I don't remember much, which is a good thing. Most of the damage was on my left side. My left leg was really battered, as was my face." She wished the big, empty room wasn't quite so bright.

"So you've had a lot of surgeries."

He wasn't asking a question but she nodded, anyway. "Dozens. For the first six months I was dealing with facial reconstruction along with my leg. I don't look the same."

He pushed away the table, his half-eaten plate of food apparently forgotten. Then he leaned toward her and gently touched her cheek. The tender gesture surprised her, especially when her first instinct was to lean into the contact.

"Does it hurt?" he asked.

"My face doesn't. There are a few tender spots, but except for a little swelling, I'm about as healed as I'm going to get there."

He studied her as if seeing her for the first time. He traced her eyebrows, then the length of her nose.

"What's different?" he asked.

They were treading on dangerous territory but she didn't know how to avoid the question. "My cheeks are a little higher and my chin is more round. The bones were completely shattered. The replacement shapes are a special plastic. Like an action figure."

He smiled faintly. "I can't picture you looking any other way."

That was good news, she thought.

"What else changed?" he asked.

"My voice is a little lower and huskier. There was some damage to the vocal chords. Obviously the most injury was done to my legs. I've been through several surgeries, and I still have a couple more to go. My goal is to be able to walk without a cane."

"Will you get there?"

She liked that he didn't offer platitudes, promising

that she would be fine when he didn't know the details of her situation. She thought about the question.

"If nothing else, I'm pretty stubborn, so I would say there's a good chance."

"I'm glad."

He was sitting very close. She hadn't noticed him moving, but suddenly he was in her personal space. Her chest tightened and her mouth got dry. She didn't know what to say or do. Her hands fluttered on her lap before she laced her fingers together to keep herself still.

She wanted him to kiss her.

The thought came from nowhere, but once it appeared, she couldn't get it out of her mind. She wanted him to pull her into his arms and kiss her. She wanted to feel his mouth on hers, to taste him again and be filled with the heat of desire.

At the same time, she wanted him to know the truth about her. She wanted him to be this close, this open and friendly and know that she was Josie Scott, his ex-wife. An impossible fantasy, she told herself.

He reached out to touch her face again. In that second she knew he *was* going to kiss her. Then, suddenly, he pulled back, shifting to his side of the sofa and reaching for his beer.

Disappointment filled her. She'd been so sure. What had happened to change his mind? Had the thought of all her injuries, surgeries and scars repulsed him? Was he concerned about getting involved with a client? Or was it something else? Make that some*one* else. She knew he was single, but there was a lot of material between not living with someone or being engaged and not being involved at all.

"I'm sure when you were first in the accident it

was hard to imagine being where you are now," he said. "This house is a little like that. Right now it's a mess, but in a few weeks you're not going to recognize it."

"I agree. It has a lot of potential."

They were changing the subject. Josie decided that she didn't mind. Maybe a few minutes of chatting about the impersonal would allow her to catch her breath.

Del looked around the main room. "I've always had a thing for this place." He grinned. "Would it shock you to know I almost bought the house with my ex-wife?"

Josie was startled—not by the information but by the fact that he would admit it. "What happened?"

He shrugged. "Some of it was money. When we were first married we didn't have enough to afford a place like this. Later, when we could have swung the loan, we couldn't seem to agree on what needed to be done." He swallowed the last of his beer. "Actually those plans I showed you are the same ones I'd had drawn up about three and a half years ago. I'd done them for Josie and me. I'm glad you liked them."

Hearing him speak her real name felt strange. As was his appreciation that she'd been in favor of his work.

"From all I've heard, you're doing so well now you could afford to buy the house on your own."

"Sure, but I guess I never made the time." He looked at her. "This place suits you. I'm glad you bought it."

"Me, too." She took in a deep breath. A question hovered on the tip of her tongue but she wasn't sure she had the courage to ask it. Or the courage to hear the answer. But it might give her the lead-in she needed to confess her identity. She squared her shoulders and plunged in with both feet. "At the risk of intruding where I'm not welcome, what went wrong in your marriage?"

Del took his time responding to the inquiry. He wasn't sure he wanted to talk about Josie. Not with a woman like Rose sitting next to him. He would rather discuss why someone as interesting and obviously intelligent as Rose wasn't married or even involved. He would rather go on at length about how attractive he found her, especially with the light catching the waves in her long, blond hair. He wanted to stare deeply into her eyes and go back to touching her pretty face. He'd come damn close to kissing her a few minutes ago. He wanted to slide next to her and this time give in to the hot need building inside of him.

But getting involved with a client wasn't smart. So he'd stopped himself before, and he would distract himself now. Even if that meant talking about Josie.

"You're nothing like her," he said by way of an answer.

Rose smiled. "I don't know if that's good or bad."

"It's good. You're a comfortable person to be around. Quiet, thoughtful. I feel relaxed. Josie was always going a hundred miles an hour. Sometimes I wanted to just sit and be." He grimaced. "That wasn't her style."

Rose touched her left leg. "She probably had a choice in the matter. I don't."

"I think you would be restful, regardless."

He found his thoughts drifting to what life had been

like with his ex-wife. To what had gone wrong. For the first time, he found himself willing to pick at the past and discuss it. Maybe because Josie had been on his mind for the past couple of weeks. A phenomenon he still couldn't explain. Or maybe it was because of Rose. He respected her. With all she'd been through during her recovery from the accident, she could have been a bitter, closed person. But she wasn't. She was a fighter. He respected that. Josie would have been throwing things and complaining about the unfairness of it all. He doubted she would have had the character to tough it out for any length of time.

Rose was feminine and delicate—something Josie could never be. Even if she'd known how, she would rather have eaten glass than given in to him. But that wasn't something he could share with the woman sitting next to him. Nor did it answer the question about what had gone wrong in his marriage.

"I met Josie when she was nineteen," he said slowly. "She was going to college and wanted a part-time job to give her spending money. The rest of her schooling was covered by a full athletic scholarship. Josie was all things physical."

Rose didn't say anything, but he felt her stiffen slightly. Only then did he understand his remark was a little insensitive. "Sorry," he said quickly.

"No, don't be. I asked because I'm curious. So she was an athlete?"

Del wasn't sure if he should keep talking or not, but when Rose nodded encouragingly, he continued.

"She was more than that. Josie was movement. She couldn't sit still, couldn't imagine a world without exercise and sports. In a weird way, her athletic prowess got in the way of her being a woman. I'm not

saying she wasn't pretty," he added hastily. "She
was very attractive. But never feminine. She hated
dresses and makeup and sexy lingerie. I guess a lot
of it comes from her background. She was raised in
Texas, on a ranch."

"More barrel racer than queen of the rodeo?" Rose
asked.

"That's her. Some of the problem was her dad.
He's a real difficult man—stubborn, opinionated. He
raised Josie to believe that emotions were a weakness
and that the only thing that mattered was winning—
be it a race, a game or an argument."

Rose gave him a slightly shaky smile. "Not exactly
good background material for a successful marriage.
No one can win all the time."

"Tell me about it. But Josie was determined to try.
I knew that, even before I married her, but we were
both pretty young and I was in love with her. I
thought we could work things out." He paused. "I
don't know what she thought about it all."

"She was in love with you," Rose told him. "It's
why most women marry."

"Maybe. But I never thought Josie was comfortable wanting to love anyone. She didn't like showing
any kind of weakness. Loving means being vulnerable."

"So she kept that side of herself from you?"

"If she even had it." He shifted so that he was
facing Rose and stretched out one arm along the back
of the sofa. "A lot of the blame for the marriage
failing is mine. I wanted a traditional wife, and that
wasn't Josie. I knew what she was when I married
her and still I tried to change her."

"So you were looking for June Cleaver?"

"Or someone like my mom," he admitted. "Pretty dumb. In the end, I didn't get her. Josie wasn't about to change for anyone—certainly not for me. She wouldn't compromise, either. She got stubborn about some things. Like doing the laundry or cleaning house. She was so concerned about only doing her half that she wouldn't start either chore unless I was right there with her, doing my half. It used to make me crazy. She got home from work before me, but she wouldn't make dinner. She said it made her feel like a slave."

He heard a soft sound and glanced at Rose. She tucked her thick blond hair behind her ear. "Josie sounds like quite a character."

"She was, but some of it was me. I was too young to know how to handle her, so I pushed back, probably more than I should have. Josie wasn't one to walk away from a fight. So things got ugly pretty fast. There were times when I wanted us both to admit we'd been wrong, but she wouldn't have any of that. She wanted me to say *I* was wrong. Even when it was obvious that the fighting was ripping us apart, she wouldn't stop."

He paused and listened to the sound of his own breathing. Talking about it like that brought back a lot of the emotions from that time in his life. He didn't like the remembering or the feelings. He'd put all aspects of his marriage behind him, yet it oddly felt so close tonight.

"At the risk of offending you," Rose said, "she sounds like a selfish person."

The statement made him mildly uncomfortable. "Maybe. Maybe it was how she was raised. All I know for sure is I wanted us to be a team, to learn

how to communicate like rational people. She
wanted…''

His voice trailed off as he realized he didn't know
what Josie had wanted from him. ''Maybe she was
too much like her father, or maybe I wanted someone
to treat me like my mom treated my dad. Maybe it
was a personality thing and we never had a chance. I
don't know. But she's gone now, and it's good that
we're apart. I have a lot of regrets from that time in
my life, but being divorced from Josie isn't one of
them.''

Rose busied herself collecting their plates and
dropping them into one of the bags. She seemed stiff,
almost embarrassed. Del wondered if he'd said too
much.

''More of an answer than you want?'' he asked.

She gave him a smile that seemed more pain than
humor. ''Not at all. I appreciate your candor.''

He wanted to believe her, but he wasn't sure he
could. ''What about you? What's your story?''

''I, um, was married before.'' She cleared her
throat. ''Nothing much happened. I guess we drifted
apart over time. Like you and your ex-wife, we were
young. Sometimes that makes things more difficult.''

Del had the sense that something was wrong. ''Did
I offend you with what I said?''

''Not at all.'' She touched a hand to her stomach.
''I'm suddenly not feeling very well. I guess it's all
the activity from the week catching up with me.''

Del immediately stood. Disappointment passed
through him. While he hadn't expected anything to
happen between them, and even though he'd been
telling himself that a personal involvement with a client was dumb, he had secretly hoped that he might

get a chance to kiss Rose. Maybe just a quick good-bye peck as he left. But he could tell from the lines of tension around her mouth and the white cast to her skin that she was very close to being ill.

"Are you going to be all right by yourself?" he asked. "Should I call a doctor?"

"No. It's not serious. I just need to rest a little. I'll be fine in the morning."

He wasn't sure he believed her, but didn't think he should push the point. So he gave her a nod and headed for the door.

"I'll be around all weekend," he said, as he paused in the foyer. "Page me if you need anything. Even if it's just to talk because you're tired of your own company."

"I will," she murmured, but he sensed she was lying. "Good night, Del. Thanks for dinner."

He hesitated before letting himself out. Waiting, he guessed, for Rose to change her mind and invite him to stay. But she didn't, so he stepped out into the night and wondered what had happened to shift things between them. Obviously, he'd said too much about Josie. But it wasn't just that, he thought as he climbed into his truck and started the engine. He had the sense of having been close to something significant and then of missing the point completely. But for the life of him he couldn't figure out what he hadn't been able to see.

Chapter Six

Josie sat on the sofa and listened to the sound of the door closing behind Del. She was glad he'd seen himself out because she wasn't in any shape to stand or walk or even pretend at social niceties. Her mind was racing, and there was a knot in her stomach the size of Montana. She felt hot and cold and mostly she felt sick.

Humiliation filled her. Sticky, thick humiliation. She wanted to run and hide. She wanted to turn back time and never have come back to Beachside Bay. She wanted to throw something, *anything* just to relieve the tension building inside of her.

She lifted her hand as if to do that, only to realize there wasn't anything worth throwing. The unused paper plates on the small, folding table in front of the sofa wouldn't be very satisfying. And if she let the

Chinese food rip across the room, she would only have to clean it up later.

"Damn," she whispered and covered her face with her hands, wishing for once that she was the crying kind. Maybe tears would help. But she couldn't force them. No matter how she strained, her eyes remained dry. She'd never been one for sob fests.

Everything hurt. Her body, her heart and especially her soul. She felt battered all the way down to her bones. How could Del have said all those things about her? Worse, how could he have thought them? Did he really think she was so blindly selfish? That she wouldn't compromise? That she'd cared more about winning than their marriage?

He'd compared her to Aaron. The memory made her shiver. She *hated* anyone thinking she was like her father, even if it was true. She made a low sound in her throat and hugged her arms to her chest. That's what hurt the most, she realized. That it was all true.

She squeezed her eyes more tightly closed. She'd been a bad wife and partner. There was no way to sugar coat reality. As much as Del's assessment ripped her apart inside, she couldn't say he was lying. She hadn't wanted to be horrible. She'd wanted to be gentle and kind and loving. She just hadn't known how.

Josie shifted until she curled up in a corner of the sofa. Memories from the past washed over her. She let them come, watching them like some strange, twisted movie of which she was the star. She wanted to turn away—to hide from the truth—but the past year had taught her there was no way to do that. If she didn't feel it all now, she would feel it all later. There was the possibility of postponement, but there was never any escape. The event, be it a therapy session or a recounting of her past, had to be endured in order for her to be healed.

Things had gone wrong from the beginning, she thought sadly. Del had been right when he'd said he wanted June Cleaver for a wife. She'd been stunned when he'd told her he expected her to do all the cooking and cleaning and to take care of him the way his mother had. She'd proudly announced that she wasn't anyone's slave and if there was going to be service provided in their house it would be to her. She'd been horrified by his insistence, and he'd been stunned by her refusal. They'd argued for days. Eventually Del had come to her with a compromise.

Josie opened her eyes and stared unseeingly at the empty room. Tonight Del had claimed that she had needed to be right, regardless of the cost to the marriage. That she hadn't been willing to bend or admit they could both be wrong. She wanted to protest that statement, to tell him that she had met him halfway. That many times she'd been the one to come up with a better way for them to do things or to get along. Except she hadn't. Not even once. She'd wanted everything to go her way.

She recalled how Del had carefully divided the chores between them. With the hindsight of years and maturity she recognized for the first time that for a man like Del—raised by a woman who had catered to his every need—offering to take over half the household chores was a big step. She saw now how he'd really listened to her complaints and had realized that he was being unreasonable. She'd resisted his division and had refused to do her share unless they were doing the work together. She'd been so worried about not doing one lick more than was necessary.

Tonight he'd accused her of being unreasonable. Of needing to win every fight. It wasn't enough for them both to have been wrong—she had to be right. She winced as she remembered screaming at him, slamming doors and walking out. Just like her father.

How she hated the comparison to Aaron. Yet she knew that his stubbornness, his strength that he'd passed on to her, were the reasons for her determination and victory in her recovery. She wouldn't have survived the past year without being so tough and unyielding. But what had served her well after the accident had been the downfall of her marriage.

I have a lot of regrets from that time in my life, but being divorced from Josie isn't one of them.

His words echoed inside her brain. She'd come back for closure. She'd come back for some kind of connection with Del and maybe to find a piece of her whole self to blend with the broken person she'd become. Yet he wasn't interested in anything like that. He'd put her behind him and had no intention of turning around for a second look. She'd been thinking they could have made it if only she'd been different. He'd been thinking he'd made a lucky escape.

She wasn't sure what to do with all this information. She felt small and ugly—as if she wasn't the kind of person anyone would want to be around. She wished she'd never bought the Miller house and was sorry she was going to have to see Del again. Josie wanted to run away. But she wouldn't. Although she hated the pain, she would endure it. She would see this situation through to wherever it ended, and

then she would move on to the next chapter of her
life. Because she wasn't a quitter.

Josie bent over and collected her cane, then rose to
her feet. She wanted to stick the leftover Chinese food
in the tiny refrigerator and then head up to bed.
Maybe she would feel less disgusted with herself in
the morning.

As she reached for the bag of food, the room
seemed to tilt and swirl. Walls shifted, furniture
moved until she was back in time…standing in the
house she and Del had bought the second year of their
marriage. She could see him walking through the
door, a bag of Chinese food in his hand. They'd been
fighting a lot lately and he'd suggested takeout as a
way of making peace. She'd been out running and
had been home long enough to shower, but not dress.

He'd taken one look at her wrapped in a towel and
nothing else. A light had flared to life in his dark eyes.
A heated flame she recognized. Instantly there was an
answering blaze in her own body. Despite all their
problems, they'd always found a way to connect on
a very physical level.

"Take it off," Del had growled at her.

For once she didn't mind taking orders from him.
Slowly, almost defiantly, she'd pulled the tucked end
free and let the length of terry cloth fall to the ground.
Slowly, proudly, she sauntered toward him, holding
his gaze with her own, stopping only when she was
within grabbing distance.

He hadn't disappointed her. He'd dropped their
dinner without a second thought and had reached for
her. Within seconds she was hauled up against him,
their mouths crushed together, their bodies straining.
He'd been instantly aroused, as had she. While he'd

teased her breasts and nipples until she'd been mad with desire, she'd managed to open his belt and unzip his jeans.

He turned so that she was pressed against the door. He grasped her bare rear with his hands and pulled her up to his waist. She wrapped her legs around his body to hold herself secure. He'd fumbled with his clothing, pushing down his jeans and briefs, then guiding himself into her. She'd been wet to his hardness, throbbing with need, begging him to take her.

They'd made love there, against the door. Wildly, impulsively. Kissing, biting, straining until she went first, leaping into the vortex of release, her strong, fast contractions pulling him over the edge as well.

Josie straightened and leaned on her cane. The memory receded, but the sensations of that night did not. She could still feel the cool of the wooden door on her bare back and Del's heat as he'd filled her. Desire made her ache in a way different from her constant pain. She forced herself to pick up the leftovers and take them to the kitchen. Once there she put them away and then headed for the stairs.

As she gazed up at what seemed like a man-made mountain she would have to climb, a sense of hopelessness settled over her. Del would never be interested in her that way. Not sexually. She'd been kidding herself about seeing any kind of interest in his eyes. But even if her greatest fantasy came true and he *did* find her appealing, what could she do about it? Her body was broken. While she was in the process of recovering, she would never be the same. She would never have the strength or flexibility she'd had before. She couldn't make love against a door. The hot, animal sex that was so a part of their marriage was lost to her forever. She would have to worry about being careful, of supporting healing body parts and weak areas. She would be so different.

Josie began to climb the stairs. With each step she reminded herself that pity was a one-way street to disaster. She was determined to keep on healing, to get better. But the memories were especially heavy tonight, as was the realization nothing would ever be the same for her again. Not with her body and not with her relationship with Del.

"Come on. You can get him out easy. He's a wimp."

Del clapped his hands as he yelled his opinion across the softball diamond. From his position on first base, he could see the "wimp" in question glaring at him.

Jason Newman, six feet five inches and well over 230 pounds of pure muscle pointed his bat at Del. "I'm taking you out, boy. Feet first. I'm gonna break your knees."

"You and what army? You bat like a girl. You're not going anywhere."

Jason's response was a growl of outrage. Del chuckled as he positioned himself to catch the easy out. Jason might play professional football, but he was lousy at softball. He was good for either a ground or fly out.

But even as the large man prepared to smack the ball toward first base, Del found his attention wandering. Not to the game, where it belonged, but to a blue-eyed woman with long wavy hair. He hadn't been able to forget Rose since he'd left her the previous night.

He told himself it was because she hadn't been feeling well and he was concerned about her being ill and alone in the house. Which was a big, fat lie. While he was concerned about her health he found himself thinking things that had nothing to do with healing and everything to do with making them both hot, sweaty and content.

She was sexy, smart and tempting as hell. Okay, she said she didn't cook, but he'd compromised over that one before. As Josie had taught him—that was why they had takeout.

Jason swung and hit the ball. It soared directly toward Del, who caught it easily.

"Third out," the pitcher yelled, motioning for the team to come off the field. Jason shook his head in disgust.

Del laughed as he jogged toward the bench. He'd scored in the last inning so he wasn't going to be up to bat anytime soon. He set his glove on the bench and went to get a bottle of water from the cooler by the chain link fence. As he pulled off the plastic wrap, a familiar movement caught his attention.

He turned away from the diamond and saw someone on the walking path that circled the entire park. The T-shirt and sweats weren't familiar, but he would recognize that blond hair, not to mention the cane and halting walk, anywhere.

Without stopping to think if it was a good idea or not, Del jogged toward her. He saw the exact moment Rose recognized him. She slowed to a halt and seemed to tense slightly. As if she wasn't sure she wanted to talk to him.

Del slowed as well. Instantly he thought of all the stupid things he'd said the night before. How he talked too much about his ex-wife. Talking about any woman while in the presence of another counted as extremely dumb by any measure.

But he kept moving toward her because he really wanted to talk to her. He'd thought he would have to wait until Monday to make an excuse to go over to the house. Last night she'd seemed as if she might be really sick, and he hadn't wanted to intrude if she needed the weekend to rest.

"How are you feeling?" he asked when he was within speaking distance. "Better this morning?"

She wore her hair back in a ponytail. Perspiration stained the neck of her white T-shirt and dotted her upper lips. Her cheeks were flushed, and she looked as if she'd been pushing herself physically.

"I'm fine," she said, giving him a smile that didn't seem to reach her eyes. "I had a good night's sleep, so I decided to get a little exercise." She motioned to her left leg. "I'm supposed to be in physical therapy several times a week and I've been neglecting that since I moved here. I have to be careful to make sure I don't lose ground."

"You don't look as if you're having much fun."

She wrinkled her nose. "I'll admit it's work, but that doesn't mean I can avoid it forever. What about you?" She glanced at his casual shorts and T-shirt. "Out jogging?"

"No. I'm playing softball." He pointed to the game in progress on the diamond. "My team's batting, but I won't be up this inning."

Confusion darkened her blue eyes. "But you don't like organized sports."

Her statement surprised him. "Who told you that?"

She took a step back and shrugged. "I mean, I didn't hear it from anyone. I just thought…" Her voice trailed off. "How long have you been playing?"

"A couple of years." He took a drink from his water bottle. "I'd been thinking about getting more physically active for a while. I jogged for a bit, but it was too boring, and I'm not really the go-to-the-gym type. So I tried team sports. I found I enjoy them a lot."

Rose had an odd expression on her face. As if she wasn't sure she believed him. "It's always nice to get out," she murmured.

"I agree." He glanced over his shoulder and saw his team was still at bat, then returned his attention to her. "Want to come watch? Afterward we all go out for pizza. You'd be welcome to come along."

Rose swallowed and took another step away from him. "That's really nice, but I can't. I don't know any of your friends and I wouldn't want to intrude."

"You wouldn't be an intrusion. You'd like everyone. I promise." He made an X over his heart.

She shook her head. "It would be too awkward. I'm not dressed and I still feel kind of strange going out into the world."

He stared at her. "Why?"

"Because of how I look."

He peered at her face. "Because you're not wearing makeup? It's Saturday. Don't women get a day off from that stuff?"

The tension left her body, leaving her relaxed. She laughed. "You don't get it, do you?"

"Not for a second. Want to explain it to me? Is this a chick thing?"

"No. It's a cane thing."

He glanced at her leg, then at the cane. "You mean because you need one to help you walk? Why would anyone care about that?"

She smiled a perfect smile. One that said he'd conquered the world for her and made him want to kiss her. But he wasn't going to. He didn't want their first kiss to be fast, impersonal and in public. Which meant he was in more trouble than he'd realized.

"I appreciate that my disability is no big deal to you," she said, "but it matters to other people. I'm not comfortable being stared at. But thanks for the invitation."

Before he could say anything else, he heard his name. He turned and saw his teammates waving him back into the game.

"Looks like you're needed," she said. "Good luck. I hope you win."

"Thanks. See you on Monday."

"Sure. Bye."

He turned and ran toward the diamond, all the while swearing under his breath. He should have asked her out. That's what he wanted. Client or no client, he wanted to spend time with Rose. He wanted to get to know everything about her. He wanted to be in the same room with her while they read or watched a movie. He wanted to kiss her and touch her and—

He turned back to wave, but she was already gone. The place where she'd stood on the path was empty. He wished she'd stayed to at least watch the game.

"Who was that?" Jason called as Del set down his water bottle and grabbed his mitt.

"A friend."

"Uh-huh. What about Jasmine?"

Del didn't reply. Jasmine was his on-again, off-again girlfriend. They were currently in off-again mode. He hadn't thought about her for days. A while back he'd been thinking of calling her, but things had changed in the relationship. He shook his head. No point in lying to himself. Nothing had changed. Instead he'd become distracted by a very attractive woman. Someone he couldn't wait to see again. If only he could think of an excuse to drop by her place tomorrow.

Del's crew showed up promptly at eight on Monday morning. Josie was grateful to let them in. Except for her brief encounter with Del in the park on Saturday, she hadn't spoken to anyone all weekend. She was tired of her own company.

She greeted the guys and ushered them into the main room where she'd already brewed a pot of coffee.

"You don't have to do this, ma'am," Jerry said as he filled a mug. "But we sure appreciate it."

She smiled. "It's not as if I have to spend my morning cleaning house or cooking." She motioned to the gutted kitchen. "It's my pleasure. Oh, and please call me Rose."

Jerry nodded his agreement. The other men poured themselves coffee, then they went to various parts of the house to get to work. Josie watched them go. She wondered if Jerry would have been as pleasant if he'd known who she really was. She remembered overhearing him talking with one of the other guys. She'd been at a construction sight, fighting with Del. Jerry had said that while she had a great butt and was probably dynamite in bed, her personality was such that he would rather try taming a wounded polar bear.

Josie leaned against her cane and admitted to herself that Jerry's assessment had been right on the money. Since arriving back in Beachside Bay she'd been getting all kinds of information about herself that she hadn't expected. Ironically she'd returned for closure but instead she was getting a life lesson in eating crow. While she didn't especially like it, it might be just what she needed.

And there were one or two bright spots. She thought Del might like her a little. While she didn't think he was interested in more than being friends or possibly a mild flirtation, it was nice to know that her altered appearance hadn't sent him screaming from the room. She still found the concept of him with another woman disquieting, but she was willing to let that go as long as the other woman was her.

The thought made her smile. The other piece of good and interesting news was that Del had taken up softball. During their three years of marriage she'd been on his case constantly, trying to get him to participate in some form of exercise. He'd resisted and yet now he was on a team. She knew that was from her influence. At least she hadn't been completely horrible—there had been one or two good things in their marriage.

She walked over to the coffee maker to start a second pot. As she moved, the pain in her left leg shot up into her hip and back. She was sore from her walk on Saturday—her own fault. She hadn't been keeping up with her exercises or her physical therapy. If she didn't start soon, she was going to pay a price. Unfortunately she wasn't motivated at the moment.

She'd worked so hard and so long and it still was not where she wanted to be. Occasionally—like now—frustration overwhelmed her good sense.

"Get over it," she said aloud, knowing she didn't have time for self-pity. She had a life to rebuild. After she made the coffee, she would go upstairs and start a list. She didn't know what for, but list-making always improved her mood.

As she poured water into the pot, using the gallon of bottled water she'd bought, the front door opened. She heard several voices. Most of them were low and masculine but one was shrill, demanding and crabby. Josie set the pot down and turned toward the sound.

Three good-looking burly construction workers walked into the main room followed by a tiny, red-headed woman in her sixties. She glanced around at the main room, then focused on the kitchen.

"It's all a mess," the woman announced planting her hands on her hips. She wore denim coveralls and a long-sleeved red T-shirt that clashed with her bright-red hair.

"Once again I'm going to have to fix everyone's mistakes." She turned to the three gorgeous twenty-something males hovering beside her. "You fellows plan on posing for a calendar or did you want to do some work?"

The three hunks jumped to attention at her question.

Josie couldn't keep herself from grinning. If she'd been able to run, she would have thrown herself into the older woman's strong arms and stayed there for-ever. Annie May wasn't just a master plumber and a force to be reckoned with, she was the closest thing to a grandmother Josie had ever had. Leaving her when Josie had left Beachside Bay had been nearly as difficult as leaving Del.

Josie took a single step toward her, then paused. She had a disguise to think of.

"You must be Rose," the older woman said, walking over and holding out her hand. "You know what you're getting into buying this place?"

Josie relished the familiar strength as Annie May shook her hand and then stepped back. "It's too late now," she said. "I'm the proud owner and, as you can see, the construction has already started."

Josie held her breath as Annie May gave her the once-over, starting at her feet and working her way to the top of her head. There wasn't even a flicker of recognition. Josie felt both relieved and sad. She would have liked a friend to confide in, but she wasn't ready to come clean with Del. After their conversation here Friday night—when he'd told her exactly what he thought of her—she was hardly in a position to reveal her past.

Annie May tilted her head slightly and motioned to her cane. "A man do that to you?"

At first Josie didn't understand. Then she got it. "No, I wasn't beat up. I was hit by a truck."

"It looks bad. The good news is you lived to talk about it. You're upright and except for buying this old place, I'm guessing you're smart enough. So you were lucky."

Josie wanted to protest. She felt anything *but* lucky. Yet in her own outspoken fashion, Annie May had zeroed in on the truth. Josie could have died in the accident. She could have lost her leg completely or be left paralyzed or facially disfigured. In the scheme of things, she'd actually gotten off pretty light.

Annie May glanced at her three helpers. "Bring in the supplies. We're going to start with the kitchen today."

"Yes, ma'am," they said in unison and left the room.

"Pretty, but not the brightest bulbs in the chandelier," Annie May said as the men walked out of the house. "Still, hiring the good-looking ones is one of the few compensations of my old age. Del accuses me of being a sexist pig, and he's right." She grinned. "So, let's talk about your kitchen. I've seen the plans. They're not too bad. I'd suggest a couple of changes, though. Seeing we're going to be running pipes anyway, why not put a deep sink in the island?"

She walked to the diagram pinned to the wall and pointed. "There's plenty of room and it would give you a second work station. Wouldn't cost very much. If you keep the house, you'll find it handy. If you sell, the buyers will appreciate it."

She walked back to the kitchen and shared a couple of other ideas. Josie listened, torn between appreciating her suggestions and wishing she could talk to Annie May. After all that had happened, she really needed a friend.

The hunks returned, and Annie May set them to work, measuring the kitchen and marking where the pipes would run. When they were busy, Annie May motioned to the parlor.

"Let's go in there. I want to show you something."

Josie followed her, wondering if the older woman was going to suggest a wet bar. Josie didn't think it would fit with the house. But what other plumbing issue could there be in the front room?

Annie May waited until Josie had stepped into the

empty room, then she closed the French door, cutting off the construction sounds from the rest of the house. She turned to Josie, planted her hands on her hips again and spoke.

"What the hell do you think you're doing, Josie Scott? Frankly this is a piss-poor excuse for a disguise. You really think you're fooling anyone?"

Chapter Seven

Josie couldn't believe it. "You know who I am?"

Annie May snorted in disgust. "Of course. I'm not a fool." The older woman peered at her face. "Okay, there are a few changes. Your cheeks and chin, but your eyes are the same. Your voice is a little lower, but you talk the same."

Relief flooded Josie. She took a step toward her friend. "I've missed you so much."

"Me, too, child."

Annie May enfolded her in her arms. Although the other woman was much shorter, she was strong and familiar, and Josie felt as if she'd come home for the first time in years.

"All right," Annie May said briskly a few seconds later when she released Josie. "I want to hear about everything that happened to you." She eyed her legs, then the cane. "You probably need to sit down. How about the front porch? We should have some privacy there.''

''Sounds perfect.''

They walked outside. The morning was sunny and warm. Josie could hear the sound of people working in the house, but they were all in the rear rooms and wouldn't be likely to overhear the conversation.

''So tell me what happened,'' Annie May said when they were seated on the top step. ''Were you really hit by a truck?''

''That sucker slammed right into me,'' Josie admitted. ''I was driving home for lunch, and suddenly it was there. The brakes failed and the driver lost control.''

Annie May frowned. ''It looks like it was bad.''

''It was. I had to have a lot of surgeries on both my face and my legs. Especially the left one.'' She touched her face. ''I have a lot of plastic in me now.''

''Then stay away from open flames or you'll melt.'' Her old friend studied her. ''What took you so long?''

Josie knew what she meant. Why had she taken so long to return to Beachside Bay. To Del. The question made her a little uncomfortable because it forced a confession she wasn't sure she was ready to make. She glanced down at her lap, then looked at Annie May.

''For the first couple of years, I didn't know I wanted to come back. I was living in Los Angeles, making my life there. I had a good job, friends. Everything seemed fine.''

Although if she were being completely honest she would have to admit that *fine* made things sound better than they'd been. She'd suffered bouts of loneliness that she couldn't explain, times when nothing in her life felt right.

"After the accident, I had a lot of recovering to do. I spent months either in the hospital or in a physical rehabilitation center. It's only in the past month that I've been able to get around with a cane. Before that I needed a wheelchair or a walker. I couldn't come back like that." She shrugged. "So I waited until I could at least be upright."

Annie May patted her hand. "Makes sense, which is more than I can say for you using a different name. What were you thinking?"

Josie flushed. "I wasn't," she admitted. "I never thought Del wouldn't recognize me. I came back to talk to him and get some things settled. But when he saw me he didn't know who I was. In that second I realized I could get to know him in a whole different way without the past coming between us. It wasn't a conscious plan—it just happened."

Annie May didn't look convinced. "You're just scared he's still mad at all the stunts you pulled."

"Maybe. I would like closure on our marriage. If Del knew who I was, he wouldn't talk to me."

"Divorce isn't closure enough?"

"I guess not." She decided to tell the truth. "After the accident I kept thinking about Del. That's why I decided to come back."

"It's hard to forget the one who got away."

Josie stiffened. "Del didn't get away. I left him."

But the words didn't sound as sure as she wanted them to. She was beginning to question her reasons for coming back. After all, what did closure really mean? She knew that Del didn't have a very high opinion of her and that he was well over her. If she'd been wondering if he had any lingering feelings for her, she'd received her answer. Shouldn't that be enough?

So why hadn't she told him the truth, and why did she have the feeling she was waiting for something else?

"Although I can't help chuckling at the thought of Del not recognizing you," Annie May said, "you're going to have to tell him the truth."

"I know. And I will."

"It's already been a couple of weeks. What are you waiting for? A major holiday?"

"I don't know. I just..." She bit her lower lip. "You were right before. I'm not ready to deal with him being angry. And he's not going to take kindly to being fooled."

"You do know that the longer this goes on the madder he's going to be."

"Yeah, I know. I still want some more time before I tell him."

Her friend's gaze narrowed. "Which means you want me to keep quiet." Annie May didn't look enthused at the prospect.

"Just for a little while. Do you mind?"

Annie May sighed. "I guess in a way it's his own fault for not being able to see the truth for himself. Which is what I'll tell him when he starts in on me. All right. I won't say anything. But don't take too long. You're only digging yourself a deeper pit with this one."

"Thanks for understanding," Josie said, giving her a hug.

Annie May held her close. "Regardless of the reason, it's good to have you back, child. The world was a little less bright with you gone.''

Josie felt an unfamiliar tightness in her chest. ''I'm sorry for not staying in touch,'' she said softly, releasing her friend and looking into her wise, brown eyes. ''I should have. I guess I was disconnecting myself from everything and everyone who reminded me of Del.''

''I understand and I forgive you. But don't do it again.''

''Yes, ma'am,'' she said meekly.

Annie May touched her cheek. ''You look tired. Are you getting enough rest?''

Josie thought about her restless nights. ''Not really.''

''Then you march yourself upstairs and take a load off. You're not going to get healthy if you're too exhausted to take care of yourself. And what about seeing a doctor? Do you need to?''

No one mothered quite like Annie May, Josie thought happily as the older woman bossed her all the way up to her bedroom. She enjoyed being fussed over and instructed to not come down until she'd had at least a two-hour nap.

When Annie May had lowered the blinds and pulled up the covers, she gave Josie a kiss on the forehead before leaving and closing the door behind her. Josie lay alone in her room and sighed with contentment. Things might not be all back to normal in her world, but having Annie May back in her life was a step in the right direction.

She rolled onto her side and closed her eyes. As she did, she felt herself straining to hear a familiar voice. She was listening for Del's arrival at the house.

He stopped by every day, and she didn't want to miss his visit.

Josie sat upright in bed and pressed the covers to her chest. Her heart thundered loudly enough to drown out the sounds of construction. Realization slammed into her, just like that truck had a year before, and the results were nearly as devastating.

She wasn't back in Beachside Bay because she wanted closure. She was back because of Del. Because deep down in her soul she'd been hoping and praying that he still cared for her. Her secret fantasy had been that he would take one look at her, open his arms and say, "Oh, honey, I've been waiting for you to come back to me. I never stopped loving you and I never will."

Del's brutally honest assessment of their marriage and her part in its failure had upset her not only because he'd hurt her feelings but because hearing it had caused the death of a dream. She could no longer secretly harbor a reconciliation fantasy.

She sank back onto her pillow and wondered what she was supposed to do now. Del wasn't still in love with her. He'd moved on with his life. Shouldn't she do the same? Put him in the past and get started with her future?

Something soft brushed against her cheek. Josie stirred, then rolled onto her back and slowly opened her eyes. Afternoon sunlight made her blink slightly as she looked up at the man bending over her. His features came into focus, making her smile.

"Del," she murmured.

The sight was so familiar, she felt immediately at peace. Her questions and worries faded until they were little more than a dream. Is that what had happened? Had she just experienced a very vivid, very strange dream?

"Hey, sleepy-head. How are you feeling?"

He sounded warm and concerned, she thought happily. It all *had* been a dream. Some hideous misfiring in her brain had made her imagine a divorce, an accident and—

He held out a light-pink-and-cream rose. "I know. It's dumb. I'll bet guys do this to you all the time. But I couldn't resist."

She frowned as she took the perfect flower. "Guys do what?"

"Bring you roses. A rose for Rose. I'm sincere, but not especially imaginative."

A rose for Rose? She blinked and realized the room around her was unfamiliar. She started to sit up but a sharp pain in her leg nearly made her cry out. And then she did want to cry, but not from physical pain. Memories returned and with them the knowledge of her current situation. The divorce and the accident hadn't been a dream. They were very real. She wasn't still married to Del and he didn't know who she was.

Disappointment filled her. She ignored it, along with the pain in her leg, and forced herself to sit up.

"How long was I asleep?" she asked.

"According to Annie May, who I saw as I came in a bit ago, about three hours. It's nearly two." He settled on the mattress, his hip bumping hers. "I guess you needed the rest."

"Three hours? I can't believe it. I never sleep during the day."

"I won't tell anyone. Now fluff up those pillows behind you and prepare to be fed. Annie May was concerned that you might not eat lunch so she made me get you a sandwich. I'm going to sit here and watch you eat it. Pretty cool, huh?''

She glanced from him to the wrapped deli sandwich, two cans of soda and several wrapped cookies sitting on her nightstand. "You didn't have to do that."

"If you can say that, you don't know Annie May very well. We all listen to her." He opened a napkin and spread it on her lap. "Apparently she's taken a shine to you. She was hovering around like a mother hen and, believe me, Annie May's not one to hover over anyone."

His comments eased some of her tension. It felt nice to be fussed over, especially by two people who had once been so important to her.

She took the sandwich he offered and unwrapped it.

"I didn't know what to get," he said. "I picked turkey because almost everyone likes that. I had them throw in mustard and mayonnaise packets so you could pick which you preferred." He leaned over and grabbed a couple of the cookies. "I thought we could share these."

"Of course." She swallowed, feeling a little self-conscious. "While I appreciate the company, Del, you don't have to stay. I'm sure you have work to do."

"Not really. As the boss, I get to set my own hours, and that includes taking breaks with attractive clients. However, I'll excuse myself for a second to get a chair. I don't want to crowd you on the bed."

With that he stood up and headed out of the room. Josie wanted to protest. She liked him sitting close to her. She liked feeling his strength and his heat. But she didn't want to seem too eager or start something she wasn't prepared to finish. Instead she used her time alone to quickly use the bathroom, splashing water on her face and brushing her teeth. When she stepped back into the bedroom, Del had already returned and sat on a folding chair with his feet stretched out in front of him.

Josie lowered herself onto the mattress and leaned against the pillows.

"Aren't you going to eat?" he asked, pointing at her untouched sandwich.

"In a bit. I'm not hungry right now, but I will be."

He frowned. "Are you taking care of yourself the way you should? I know it's none of my business, but I want you to answer the question, anyway."

That made her smile. "I'm fine. I need to get back into physical therapy. My leg's been hurting a lot and I'm tired more than I should be, so I probably need to get that checked out. But I've had so many surgeries that my body is in a constant state of repair."

He popped open one of the cans of soda and took a drink. "Did your walk on Saturday help or hurt?"

She rubbed her leg. "I don't know. It's still sore. Recovery is a tricky process. Sometimes I feel as if I'm going backward more than forward."

He nodded. "It was nice to see you at the park. I wish you'd stayed for the game."

Josie opened her mouth, then closed it. She didn't know what to say. Del had opened the blinds when he'd returned, and sunlight filled the room. Several rays caught the side of his head, making his dark hair gleam. She saw flashes of dark-red and auburn among the brown-black strands. Today he wore a navy

T-shirt tucked into jeans. The soft cotton hugged his impressive muscles, emphasizing his broad shoulders and sculpted chest.

He was physically perfect. She'd never thought about it before, but of course it was true. She was intimately familiar with his body. She knew the elegant lines and hard contours.

He'd wanted her to stay for the game. She knew there was no way she could have done that. People would have stared and maybe even asked questions. Most of the time that didn't bother her, but with Del nearby, she would have worried about what he was thinking. At times he seemed to forget there was something wrong with her. She didn't need circumstances to remind him.

"I would have liked it, too," she said cautiously. "But I wasn't up to it…physically, I mean."

"I understand." He stared at her face. "If that's all it is. I'd thought maybe it might be because of what I said about my ex-wife the night before."

Embarrassment cut through her, making her face flame. She busied herself opening her own can of soda. "No. Why would that be a problem?"

"Because I said too much. I rarely talk about my marriage or my divorce. I guess once I got started, it all sort of spilled out. I made her sound like the wicked witch of the west, which isn't fair. Plus—" He leaned toward her, resting his elbows on his knees. "The way I ranted and all, I didn't want you to think there was still anything between us. I'm really over her."

"Oh, good," she managed.

Josie felt weak with humiliation. She hadn't

thought it could get worse with Del, yet here it was, falling apart even more.

He sighed. "I'm saying this all wrong. She's not a bad person. I didn't mean to imply that. She was always honest and prompt."

If she'd been able to get up and run, Josie would have done it in a microsecond. Down the stairs and out of the house, never to be heard from again. Honest and prompt? Was that the best he could do? His attempts to make her feel better were falling far short of the mark.

"You make her sound like a German shepherd," she said with a little more force than she would have liked. "Could she fetch the paper, too?"

Del straightened. "I'm making a mess of this, aren't I?"

She wanted to scream "Yes!" but didn't. Instead she sipped her drink and tried to calm down.

"Josie was a lot of good things," he said carefully. "She was fearless about physical danger and always pushed herself. If there was a sport she wasn't good at, she worked until she excelled. She didn't care about the time, the energy or the pain. She just went for it."

Josie didn't want to hear this, either. If she'd been physically capable of curling up in a small ball and hugging her knees to her chest, she would have done it. His words made her feel small and broken. The few things Del still admired about her were tied to a body she didn't have anymore. She was an idiot to have come back to Beachside Bay. Better to have stayed in Los Angeles and forgotten all about him.

But she couldn't curl up and she couldn't run. So she forced herself to shift so that she was sitting on the side of the bed. She put her can of soda on the nightstand.

"She sounds like quite an athlete," she told him. "All that exercise. She must have been in great shape."

"She was. Josie probably could have taken me if she'd tried."

He grinned as he spoke. She tried to smile, as well.

"At least your sex life was great," she said, thinking it was a small consolation, but at this point she was going to take whatever she could get.

Del didn't say anything. It took her a couple of seconds to realize he seemed very interested in his soda and wasn't responding to her statement. Her stomach dropped to her toes and every last ounce of self-worth evaporated like mist in the sun.

"Don't tell me that was horrible, too," she blurted before she could stop herself.

"Not horrible," he said quickly. "It was fine. At times it was even amazing. It's just..." His voice trailed off.

She wanted to die. Right there, sitting on the side of the bed. She wanted the world to end and take her along. She wanted to be anywhere but here, hearing anything but this. It was too much. How could he be saying the sex hadn't been fabulous? Didn't he remember all the things they'd done together? She'd always been open to new positions and new places. She'd been strong and limber, a combination he'd claimed to appreciate. Had he been lying?

"I'm not sure how to explain this," he said slowly, avoiding her gaze.

She wanted to tell him not to bother, but she was afraid if she spoke, her voice would crack. Then he would want to know what was wrong, and she couldn't think of any response to that.

"Josie was physically perfect and we had sex a lot. Most of the time it was everything a man could ask for. But sometimes it was empty."

She blinked. "Empty? I don't understand."

Del shifted uncomfortably. As if he were embarrassed. "I know guys are supposed to be into quantity rather than quality, but it wasn't like that for me. There were times I wanted to be tender and she didn't. Josie wasn't one to cuddle. She wasn't into emotional connection. We had sex a lot, but we rarely made love."

Worse and worse, she thought, too stunned to do more than keep breathing through the pain. He'd laid her bare and found her wanting in every aspect possible. For the first time in a long time, she found herself fighting tears. She who never cried. But this wound went too deep. It cut down to the very essence of her being, hurting her more than any of her surgeries. She had nothing left. She'd been an awful wife, a lousy lover and a horrible person. Why had he ever married her?

She wanted to excuse herself, but she knew she didn't have the strength to walk away. Even her cane couldn't help because her legs felt as if they would never support her weight again. She'd been so incredibly stupid to come back. She'd been harboring secret fantasies about her ex-husband while he'd been counting his blessings at getting rid of her.

Del watched the play of emotions across Rose's face. She looked unnerved by what he'd said. Smooth, he thought grimly. Once again he'd blown it. Here he was with a beautiful woman, and how was he spending his time? Trashing his ex-wife. Could he be any more stupid?

"I'm sorry," he said quickly. "That was insensitive and probably more information than you wanted."

"No," she said, her low voice a little thick. "It's not that. I was just wondering what my ex-husband says when he talks about me."

"I'm sure his opinion is completely different," he assured her. "Because you're different. I know we haven't known each other long, Rose, but you're nothing like my ex. You're warm, caring, funny, gentle and very beautiful."

She looked at him. Surprise filled her blue eyes. "You can't mean any of that."

"I mean every word."

She tucked a strand of hair behind her ear, then motioned to her legs. "I use a cane. I limp. There are scars everywhere. That's not beautiful."

Without planning the movement, he set his soda can on the floor and crossed to the bed. After sitting next to her, he turned so he could touch her face. As he stroked her cheek, he smiled.

"Can't you see your injuries don't matter? You *are* beautiful. It's not just your face, but all of you."

She parted her lips, but didn't speak. They were so close. Her scent, the promise of her curves all called to him. He told himself to get away before he did something stupid. Not something he would regret, but definitely out of line for a contractor-client relationship.

But he didn't want to stand and walk away from her. He wanted to be closer. He *needed* to feel her against him.

Slowly, so she would know what he was doing and have time to protest, he slipped his free hand around to rest on her back. He gently urged her forward, leaning into her at the same time. Carefully, deliberately, he lowered his mouth to hers. At the last second he paused, waiting for her to push him away.

Instead she touched his lips with hers.

She was soft and sweet, and he wanted to claim her instantly. Instead he forced himself to hold back. He kissed her gently, brushing against her tenderly. As he wrapped both his arms around her he was careful not to make any sudden movements. He knew that she spent a lot of her day in pain, and he wasn't sure what parts of her might be tender.

He inhaled, breathing in the scent of her shampoo and floral perfume. There was another fragrance. Something subtle he couldn't identify. It tugged at the corners of his mind in an almost familiar way. Something…

He forced the questions away. He didn't want to think about anything but Rose. He brushed his mouth against hers, back and forth, exploring her, feeling her respond to him. Her breathing quickened. Her hands rested on his shoulders, then slid down his back. When she pulled him against her, he went willingly, wanting to feel her full breasts flatten against his chest.

With his eyes closed, his other senses sharpened. Desire grew inside of him. He lightly licked her bottom lip, testing to see if she wanted the kiss to continue. When her mouth parted for him, he felt a jolt of heat in his groin. Blood rushed south, making him uncomfortably aware of his need.

He slipped his tongue between her lips. As he did,

he found his hands moving up and down her back in a way that was almost familiar. One of her hands moved up until her fingers tunneled through his hair. There was a rhythm to their movements. A familiar rhythm. Although he knew he was kissing Rose he was suddenly reminded of Josie.

Damn. Del opened his eyes to orient himself. He was with Rose. He was in her bedroom, kissing her. What the hell was Josie doing in his head?

He deepened the kiss in an effort to chase his ex-wife from his mind. In the three years she'd been gone, he'd never once thought of her while kissing another woman. But he was thinking of her now.

Rose, he told himself. Only Rose. The bodies were completely different. Rose was all curves—full breasts and hips. Her face, her hair, all of her. Rose.

Josie.

The thought intruded, breaking his concentration. Suddenly it was Josie's taste, her scent, filling his mind. He broke the kiss and stumbled to his feet. Rose opened her eyes and looked at him. Those eyes. So blue. So much like Josie's.

Anger and confusion filled him. Nothing made sense. He stared down at the woman in front of him, taking in her long, blond hair, her full, suddenly familiar mouth.

"Who are you?" he growled. "Who the hell are you?"

Chapter Eight

The question echoed in Josie's ears. *Who are you?*

She heard the words, understood their meaning, but she couldn't speak. She was too stunned by the shock she felt from the impact of Del's kiss. Too overwhelmed by passion, the past and her own realization that nothing was as she'd thought it would be.

She'd known Del was going to kiss her, even before he'd gathered her close and pressed his mouth to hers. Even through her pain at his latest revelation about their failed marriage, she'd recognized the light of need in his eyes, the desire and wanting in his expression. She'd allowed him to pull her against him because she'd needed something to ease her pain.

She'd thought that kissing him might help to make her feel better. She'd also thought it might be nice to know if there was still some passion between them. She'd expected to enjoy the contact, but she hadn't thought she would be swept away. Nor had she expected to find an unwelcome truth.

He repeated his question and she tried to answer. But she couldn't speak. She was too caught up in what she'd learned. She hadn't come back to Beachside Bay because she wanted closure. She'd come back because when she'd thought she was dying, Del was the one person she'd been thinking about. She'd come back because she was still in love with him.

The implications of that—being in love with a man who regretted every second of their marriage—nearly overwhelmed her. Her legs began to tremble as a great weakness swept through her body. Her pulse felt fast and faint at the same time.

No, not that. She couldn't still be in love with Del. It wasn't possible. It wasn't fair. He hated her, or at least despised her. He thought she was selfish, stubborn and lousy in bed. The only thing he respected about her was a body she no longer controlled.

She wanted to run away, to hide forever. She wanted to distract him or make up some other lie. Instead she squared her shoulders and forced herself to look at him. She was done with pretending. The time had come to face a situation entirely of her own making.

"I'm Josie," she said. "I know I look and sound different, but that's because of the accident."

Del shook his head in denial. Josie? His Josie? He stared at the woman sitting in front of him and tried to find some piece of the woman he'd known...and married. His mind reeled as he attempted to believe what she was saying. His senses—the ones engaged during the kiss—told him she was telling the truth. The rest of him refused to believe it.

"Josie?"

Was it possible? He studied the unfamiliar face, looking for a trace of the woman he'd lived with for three years. He searched her eyes, accepting the color and shape was the same. Her mouth, too. But the rest of her? He shook his head. Everything had changed. Her cheeks, her chin, her hair. Her body.

He swore under his breath as he looked—really *looked*—at her body. A couple of faint scars were visible on her forearm. The soft cotton dress she wore outlined full breasts and hips so incredibly foreign from what he remembered. Her cane lay on the floor. A cane? Josie? Having to walk with help? A woman who had spent her entire life running and jumping and searching for the next physical challenge.

"You can't be," he said.

"If you're caught up in the physical changes, I have trouble accepting them myself," she said quietly, her voice low and unfamiliar.

He took another step back. "But you don't just look different, you sound different."

"I know. There was minor damage to my vocal cords. Nothing serious, but it changed the pitch of my voice."

She was so damned calm and rational. As some of the shock wore off, anger seeped into him. Anger and rage and a sense of having been played for a fool.

"What kind of game is this?" he demanded. "What did you think you were doing, lying to me? Is this a joke?"

He glared at her, demanding answers. The old Josie would have pushed back, harder and longer, turning things around so everything was his fault. But this new Josie—a woman he couldn't connect with the one he'd known before—simply shook her head.

"I don't have a good response to that," she admitted, not quite meeting his eyes.

"That's not good enough. What do you want? Why did you come back here?"

She swallowed. If he hadn't known better, he would swear that she was hurt and more than a little scared. But that wasn't possible. Nothing scared Josie and she didn't care about anyone enough to get hurt. She only cared about herself and winning.

He pulled out the chair he'd sat in before and slumped heavily in the seat. He couldn't get a handle on all the new information. Because the woman he'd known before had nothing in common with the woman he'd gotten to know over the past few weeks. Delicate, pretty Rose with the flowing dresses and long wavy hair was nothing like his ex-wife. Not in looks, attitude or personality.

"I'm not sure why I came back," she said slowly, finally looking at him. "There was an assortment of reasons, none of which I can explain right now. I didn't set out to trick you. I honestly thought you'd recognize me when you saw me."

"But I didn't and you didn't say anything."

"I know." She dropped her gaze to her hands. They twisted together on her lap as she laced and unlaced her fingers.

"Why did you do it? What did you have to gain by being Rose?"

"It wasn't about gain. It was about…" She sighed. "You liked Rose a whole lot more than you liked me. It was dumb, I know, but I thought that maybe if I was someone else, we could sort of get to know each other again. As different people."

He stiffened, disbelief fueling his anger again. Yeah, right. On what planet would Josie Fitzgerald want a second chance with anyone? She was lying to him again, damn her. Playing some kind of twisted game.

"Why would you think I'd want to get to know you again?" he asked, being deliberately cruel. "One relationship with you was enough. I might be a slow learner, but I figured out that lesson. Once with you was plenty."

She made a sound low in her throat. He wasn't impressed by the trick, so he ignored it. Josie reached for her cane, then rose to her feet. Her movements were shaky and awkward. For a second he wondered if she was all right, then he pushed the concern away. He didn't give a rat about her. He'd already fallen for the "poor me" game once. He wasn't going to do it again. For all he knew, there wasn't a damn thing wrong with her.

"I'm sorry," she whispered, dropping her head so that her hair swung down, shielding her face from view.

But not before he saw a glint that on anyone else he would have sworn was a tear. Except Josie never cried. Not once in all the time he'd known her.

"I c-can't do this anymore," she said, walking haltingly toward the door. "I'm sorry. About everything. I just can't."

She sounded broken and in pain. He almost weakened. Then he reminded himself what she'd been doing for the past three weeks, how he'd been attracted to her and had imagined her to be someone he would like to know better. The rage returned, and with it his resolve to stand firm.

"You're not leaving," he said as he stood. "Not until we get this settled. For once, we're going to finish a conversation. You're not going to run out or throw something. You're going to stand right here until this is resolved."

She raised her head and stared at him. Tears swam in her eyes. Josie crying?

"Please, Del," she begged. "Don't make this any more horrible. You've already told me exactly what you think of me. Do you really have to torture me any more?"

He remembered then all the things he'd told "Rose" about his ex-wife. The brutal assessments of her personality and how she'd disappointed him both in and out of bed. He winced, knowing that would have been tough for anyone to hear. Then he reminded himself he'd only spoken the truth. If Josie wasn't strong enough to hear it, that wasn't his fault. He would—

"Del?"

The soft sound cut through his thoughts. She swayed slightly. Instantly he knew something was wrong. Really wrong. But before he could reach her, she collapsed on the floor.

Four hours later Del stood at the foot of Josie's hospital bed watching a nurse take her vital signs. He hadn't thought the situation between them could get anymore strange, but he'd been wrong.

According to the emergency room doctor who had admitted Josie, she was dehydrated, fighting an infection and generally run-down. Del felt as if he were somehow responsible—as if their argument had been what had pushed her over the edge. She'd regained consciousness almost immediately after one of his crew had called 911, but Del would never forget those few minutes of panic when he hadn't been sure if she were dead or alive.

Nothing made sense, he thought as the nurse finished her work, gave him a reassuring smile and left the room. How could this woman who looked and acted so differently be his ex-wife? And he knew she was Josie. She'd been through a horrible experience and had survived.

He felt a flash of guilt. While they'd been arguing at her house, he'd wondered if she'd made up the accident. But once in the hospital she'd changed from her regular clothes to a hospital gown. As she'd been sliding into bed he'd seen the scars crisscrossing her legs. Some were thin and faded but others appeared to be recent. He recalled that, as Rose, she'd told him there was more surgery in her future.

Who are you?

He wanted to ask the question again, but this time without the anger. He really wanted to know who she had become. Was Rose real? Not the name, of course, but the woman behind the name. Is that why he'd been so angry? Was it so much about Josie's lies or had he been regretting the loss of someone he'd been starting to care about?

Who was real? The old Josie or the new Josie? Had her ''Rose'' personality been a reflection of the changes in her life or was it all an act?

''What are you thinking?''

He looked up and saw Josie watching him with a wary expression. Despite the confusion and the questions, he couldn't help smiling ruefully. "At least I understand why the more I was around Rose, the more I thought of you. I couldn't figure out what was going on. After three years you were firmly back in my brain, and I didn't know why."

He also understood the attraction he felt for Rose. Whatever their other problems, there had always been chemistry between Josie and him. Although, he wasn't going to share that with her.

"At least I did what you said," she told him, pushing on the hospital bed controls so she sat in a more upright position. "I didn't walk out on the fight." She gave a little shrug. "I think that's a first."

"Your exit was quieter, but no less dramatic. If I have to pick, I would prefer you to walk out. Or even throw something. When you passed out I was terrified I'd killed you."

The corners of her mouth twitched up slightly. "I'm made of sturdier stuff than that. Obviously, or I wouldn't have survived the accident."

He didn't know what to say to that. Josie's strength had never been something he would question. He was surprised that she'd endured as much as she had and still kept her sense of humor.

She looked at him then. Her blue eyes carefully blank, all trace of emotions—and tears—cleared away. "You don't have to stay. I appreciate that you came with me in the ambulance, but I'll be fine. I know the drill."

Part of him wanted to go, but he couldn't seem to make his feet move toward the door. Instead he pulled one of the chairs for visitors to the side of her bed and sat down.

An Important Message from the Editors

Dear Reader,

Because you've chosen to read one of our fine romance novels, we'd like to say "thank you!" And, as a <u>special</u> way to thank you, we've selected <u>two more</u> of the books you love so well, <u>plus</u> an exciting mystery gift, to send you absolutely FREE!

Please enjoy them with our compliments...

Rebecca Pearson

Editor

P.S. And because we <u>value</u> our customers, we've attached something extra inside...

EDITOR'S FREE GIFT SEAL · THANK YOU

Peel off seal and Place inside...

How to validate your
Editor's FREE GIFT "Thank You"

1. Peel off gift seal from front cover. Place it in space provided at right. This automatically entitles you to receive 2 FREE BOOKS and a fabulous mystery gift.

2. Send back this card and you'll get 2 brand-new Silhouette Special Edition® novels. These books have a cover price of $4.50 each in the U.S. and $5.25 each in Canada, but they are yours to keep absolutely free.

3. There's no catch. You're under no obligation to buy anything. We charge nothing—ZERO—for your first shipment. And you don't have to make any minimum number of purchases—not even one!

4. The fact is, thousands of readers enjoy receiving their books by mail from the Silhouette Reader Service™. They enjoy the convenience of home delivery...they like getting the best new novels at discount prices BEFORE they're available in stores...and they love their *Heart to Heart* subscriber newsletter featuring author news, horoscopes, recipes, book reviews and much more!

5. We hope that after receiving your free books you'll want to remain a subscriber. But the choice is yours—to continue or cancel, any time at all! So why not take us up on our invitation, with no risk of any kind. You'll be glad you did!

6. Don't forget to detach your FREE BOOKMARK. And remember...just for validating your Editor's Free Gift Offer, we'll send you THREE gifts, *ABSOLUTELY FREE!*

GET A FREE MYSTERY GIFT..

YOURS
FREE!

**SURPRISE MYSTERY GIFT
COULD BE YOURS _FREE_
AS A SPECIAL
"THANK YOU" FROM
THE EDITORS OF SILHOUETTE**

Visit us online at
www.eHarlequin.com

"How many times have you been through this before?" he asked.

"This is my first collapse, if that's what you're asking. As for hospital stays…I've lost count."

She spoke calmly, as if sharing her thoughts on the weather. He couldn't imagine the Josie he knew enduring endless days of inactivity while her body healed. Had she not raged against the constraints, the pain, the slow progress? But as he looked at her he realized she wasn't the Josie he knew.

Everything about her was different. The long, wavy hair, the different facial features. She wore makeup and dresses. He wasn't sure there was anything of the old Josie left. Worse, he wasn't sure he wanted there to be. As much as he hated to admit it, he'd liked the new Josie very much. Maybe too much.

"This is pretty confusing," he said into the silence. "I don't know what to think."

"I'll bet. There are times when I look in the mirror and give myself a fright. And I've had months to get used to what I look like. You've only had a few hours." She pleated the sheets between her fingers. "I really didn't plan on keeping it a secret, Del. That just happened. I'm not saying it was right, but I didn't do it out of malice."

"I know."

Despite his earlier accusations, he knew that she wouldn't have gone to all this trouble to trick him. Josie was many things, but she wasn't subtle. When she wanted something, she went after it with all the energy at her disposal. When she had a problem with a person, she confronted that person directly.

"I thought you would recognize me," she continued, then glanced at him from under her lashes. "Annie May did."

He groaned. "Great. And she didn't say a word."

"I asked her not to. Besides, she just saw me this morning. She might have decided to come clean."

"Maybe."

But he doubted it. Josie and Annie May had always been close.

"I didn't want you to feel sorry for me," she whispered. "I can stand anything but that."

Without stopping to consider his actions, he moved closer to the bed. "I could never pity you, Josie. You're way too tough for that."

"I'm not very tough right now."

He wasn't going to agree with her, even if it was true. Instead he reached up and touched her long hair. "You let it grow. I never knew you had waves. I like it."

"Thanks. I didn't know about the waves, either. I always wore my hair really short. After the accident, getting it cut was the least of my problems and suddenly it was long." She tucked her hair behind her ears. "On days when I can't move around much, fixing my hair gives me something to do. When I'm feeling strong, I can get it out of the way by putting it back in a ponytail, so it works."

Josie was tall and strong and vibrantly alive. At least she used to be. He couldn't reconcile that image with the pale woman sitting in the hospital bed. Two IV lines dripped into her arm. She was wearing a hospital gown. His Josie? Never.

"What about the other changes?" he asked. "You wear dresses now instead of jeans. Except on your walk last Saturday. Then you wore sweats."

She sighed. "Jeans are too hard. Most days my legs don't work that well. There's a lot of pain from the surgeries. It's just easier to pull a dress over my head and go."

"I'm sorry for the reason, but I like you in dresses. You're very pretty and feminine in them."

"Not at all like the old me, huh? No wonder you didn't recognize me."

No wonder at all, he thought. She couldn't run anymore or play basketball. "Are you working?" Last he'd heard she'd been a PE teacher and coach at a private girls' high school in Los Angeles.

"Not since the accident. Eventually I'm going to have to do something but right now I'm not sure what."

He stared at her, at the changes. "I can't believe this is really you."

She gave him a bright smile that was as fake as plastic wood. "It's amazing what a close encounter with a big truck will do," she said brightly. "You should have seen me the first couple of months. My face and most of the left side of my body was either bandaged or covered with a cast. I looked like mummy woman for what felt like weeks. There were braces and therapy sessions, surgeries, months in rehab. You name it, I did it. You remember my stepsister, Dallas?"

He nodded.

"She and I shared an apartment together in West Los Angeles. She's a grad student at UCLA. The timing turned out to be terrific. I had a few weeks at home in between surgeries which coincided with her summer break. By the time she had to return to school, I was back in the hospital."

He believed everything she was saying and yet it was like listening to someone talk about a movie they'd seen. No real person could have gone through this and survived. "And it's really been a year?"

She nodded. "It was a year last month."

He should have known, he thought suddenly. He should have sensed something was wrong with Josie. "I wish you'd had someone get in touch with me."

Her blue gaze met his with a directness he remembered. "Why? What difference would it have made?"

"I would have come to be with you. Or does your family dislike me so much that they didn't want me there?"

"They like you just fine. The reason they didn't contact you was that I told them not to. We'd been divorced for two years."

"But—"

She cut him off with a shake of her head. "Would you have let me know if the situation had been reversed? Would you have wanted me with you?"

"That's different."

"That's also your way of saying no."

"But I'm not the point. You are. Your not getting in touch with me had nothing to do with the divorce. You would have hated needing me. That's why you couldn't do it. You never wanted to need anyone."

He couldn't keep the bitterness out of his voice. Josie's independent streak had been something he'd admired at the beginning of the marriage, but by the end, he'd grown to hate it. She would rather have eaten glass than admit she needed anyone for anything.

"Maybe once," she admitted. "But not anymore. The last year has taught me that I do need people and

I'm going to need them for the rest of my life. There were days when I couldn't even feed myself. Believe me, I learned all about being dependent then.''

"That's different.''

"I don't think it is. For a long time I thought I was strong because I was physically capable, but I've learned that being strong is about will and determination. I could have given up, but I didn't—no matter how much the odds were against me or how much it hurt. I experienced the worst it could be and I survived.''

"I'm not questioning your strength.'' He straightened, shifting the chair back a little. "You've always been stubborn.''

She shook her head. "I'm different, Del. You have to know that. If I'd been the same you wouldn't have been interested in getting to know Rose.''

"How much of Rose was real and how much of it was a game?'' He couldn't keep the anger out of his voice. "You were playing with me.''

"No. It was all very real.''

He wanted to believe her. He wanted to know that she was different, which was crazy because he wasn't interested in reigniting the flame with his ex-wife.

"I need some time to think about this,'' he said, standing, "and you need some rest.''

She tilted her head as she looked up at him. "It's strange. For the first time since I've known you, you're the one walking away, not me.''

"I guess I've changed, too. I'll be back in the morning.''

"You don't have to.''

"Yes, I do. Do you want me to call your folks and let them know you're in the hospital?''

"No. I'm only going to be here a couple of days.
I don't want anyone worrying."

More than likely she didn't want them hanging
around. As he'd said before—Josie hated needing
anyone. Then, because he didn't know what else to
say, he turned on his heel and left.

Chapter Nine

Nothing made sense, Del thought as he headed down the hospital corridor. Rose, Josie...which one was real? How could his ex-wife be so different? Intellectually he knew about the accident and the surgeries, but in his heart, he didn't believe it. She couldn't have gone through all that and survived. And having survived, he doubted she could have changed all that much. She might look physically different, but on the inside, where it mattered, he would bet she was exactly the same.

"Mr. Scott?"

He'd almost reached the elevator when he heard someone calling his name. He turned and saw a short woman with dark hair and glasses. She wore a white coat and had a patient chart in her hands.

"I'm Del Scott," he said.

"I thought you might be." The woman gave him

a smile, then held out her free hand. "I'm Dr. Sanders. I've examined Josie and will be taking care of her while she's here in the hospital."

Dr. Sanders looked to be in her mid-forties. She was pretty, in a capable-looking way, with blue-gray eyes and a steady gaze that seemed to see down to his soul.

After they shook hands, she gestured to a small empty office just off the main corridor. "Do you have a minute? I need to clear up a few things."

"Sure."

He followed her into the consulting room and took the visitor's chair, leaving the seat behind the metal desk for her. When she was seated, she studied the top sheet on the chart, then turned her attention to him.

"I've spoken with Josie. I have a summary of her procedures over the past year. According to her, she's divorced. You two share the same last name. Am I correct in assuming you're her ex-husband?"

He nodded, not sure what this had to do with anything.

"I see. Well, that lets you off the hook, doesn't it."

What was she talking about? "I don't understand."

"Ms. Scott hasn't been taking care of herself as well as she should. Her stay here is the result of that. She will require some specific care when she leaves us, but if you're not married, it's not your problem."

She was right. Josie wasn't his problem. She hadn't been for years. Basically the doctor was telling him it was all right to walk away. To forget this ever happened. Del sucked in a deep breath. Except it wasn't going to be that easy. Not that he should be surprised. Nothing with Josie was ever easy.

"She came back to town a few weeks ago," he said. "She bought a house and I'm remodeling it for her. So we've been spending a lot of time in each other's company."

He was deliberately making it sound as if they were considering a reconciliation. Which was crazy. He didn't want anything more to do with her. But he also knew he couldn't just walk away and forget what had happened. Somehow, without him being aware of how or when or anything, his ex-wife had reentered his life. She'd caught his attention in a way he wouldn't have thought possible, pretending to be someone else. And he'd never even come close to guessing the truth. The only hint had been that when he was around her, he couldn't stop thinking about Josie.

"So you're considering a reconciliation?" the doctor asked.

"We haven't gotten that far," he said, not willing to outright lie. "But we do have a history, and I'm concerned about her. I don't know all the details of her accident and recovery. I know it's been grueling."

"Does Ms. Scott have other family in the area?"

"No. Her folks live in Texas. She has a brother up in Seattle and a stepsister in Los Angeles. I'm the only one in town."

Dr. Sanders tapped her pen against the chart. "This makes things more difficult."

"Why?"

She leaned forward, her gaze direct. "Your ex-wife has let a few things slide. For some patients, that's fine, but for her, in her stage of recovery, it was a mistake. She hasn't been getting enough rest, which interferes with the body's ability to heal. In addition to being dehydrated, she has a low-grade infection. Due to her lack of physical therapy, her muscles are weakening. Unfortunately, she's about to pay for her personal neglect. She's going to have to spend the next few weeks in a wheelchair. She will be allowed to stand on her own for short periods of time so she can shower without assistance, but other than that, she's to be sitting or lying down. In addition, she can't drive until I've cleared her.''

Del heard the words but he didn't believe them. A wheelchair? Josie? She would hate that. Anyone would. The restrictions on her life, the dependency.

"You look shocked," Dr. Sanders said.

"I am. Stunned."

An odd expression crossed the woman's face. "Mr. Scott, this isn't the first time your ex-wife has been in a wheelchair. According to her medical history, she's only been able to use a cane full-time for about two months."

Was that possible? Had Josie really been so disabled for so long? He'd heard her talk about her surgeries and the recoveries, but he hadn't understood it before.

"You said you were remodeling a house for Ms. Scott. Is it going to be compatible with the change in her condition?"

A wheelchair at the old Miller place? He pictured the empty rooms and all the construction equipment and supplies. He thought about the drop cloths on the floors and the fact that the only bedroom was upstairs.

"I can tell from your expression that there are going to be problems,'' the doctor said. ''Should I call a family member?''

He knew what she was asking. It would be easy for him to say yes, to dump the responsibility on someone else. He and Josie were divorced. He hadn't asked her to come back, and he sure didn't want anything resembling a reconciliation. He'd done fine without her all this time.

But he also wasn't willing to turn his back on her. For reasons he couldn't explain, he felt he owed her more than that.

''You don't have to call anyone else,'' he said. ''I'll be responsible.''

''I see. Will your ex-wife agree to this?''

He couldn't help smiling. ''I suspect Josie will put up a bit of a fight, but in the end, she's not going to have another choice. I can't see her running home after all this time. The rest of her family have their own lives. No, this is for the best.''

''If you're sure,'' Dr. Sanders said. ''I will be providing you with a list of instructions, including exercises she has to do every day. Also, I'm putting her back into physical therapy to help her build up her strength and her range of motion. She has to do these things or she will lose her ability to walk. It's not going to be easy.''

Of course, he thought ironically. Why would this be any different from any other situation with Josie. ''Easy?'' he said. ''Nothing is ever easy with her.''

He found Annie May on her knees in Josie's empty kitchen, cutting into the wall and cursing to high heaven.

''We have to talk,'' he said abruptly.

"Go away. I'm busy."

"I know about Josie."

Annie May set her small saw on the floor and turned to face him. Most of the crew had left for the day so they were alone, except for one guy patching a wall on the second floor. She stood up, all five-foot-nothing of her and planted her hands on her hips.

Her coveralls dwarfed her slight frame, and her red hair glowed like fire. She was intelligent, mouthy and hell on wheels when her temper got the better of her. But this time she was the one in the wrong.

"How is she?" Annie May asked.

"Fine."

She shifted slightly. "You look mad. Guess you figured out the truth, huh?"

"Yes. Why didn't you tell me?"

Thin red eyebrows drew together. "For one thing I just found out this morning when I saw her for the first time since she'd been back. For another thing, she's your wife. Seems to me you would have recognized her."

"She *was* my wife. We've been divorced for three years. And she looks completely different."

"I knew who she was in a hot minute."

He ignored that. "You took her side. You've known me nearly all my life, and yet when I showed up here today you didn't even hint at the truth." He hated that Annie May's actions left him feeling betrayed. He'd known that she and Josie had been close, but Josie had walked away from all of them, including Annie May.

The older woman sighed. Her hands dropped to her sides. "I know. I felt real bad about that, too."

"Not bad enough."

She glared at him. "Don't be talking to me that way. You might be nearly twice my size, but that don't mean spit and we both know it." Some of her tension eased as she shrugged. "Dammit, Del, what do you want from me? I did what I thought was best. When I saw Josie, I was happy she was back. I'd missed her. I always liked her, and I felt bad for her. You were so bent on making sure she knew everything that went wrong in the marriage was her fault."

He couldn't believe it. "How can you say that?"

Annie May's gaze sharpened. "It takes two to tango. Always has. So the problems in the marriage were shared, at least in my mind. You don't have to agree if you don't want to."

Her tone clearly stated that if he didn't agree, he was a fool. Del didn't think anything could shock him, but this did.

"It wasn't me," he protested, knowing even as he spoke that he was yelling into the wind. "She was the one who wouldn't compromise. What about all the times I suggested we share responsibilities? From the cooking to the laundry, I was willing to do half. Sometimes more. But she wanted it all her way or not at all. What about all the times she wouldn't admit she was in the wrong? It could never be both of us. In her mind I had to be the one to crawl or it didn't count."

Annie May dismissed him with a wave. "I'm not saying she was a saint. Josie's many things, but perfect isn't one of them. She's as stubborn and difficult as you. But that's my point. You're just as pigheaded, only you never wanted to see that. It was always easier to talk about compromise and make all the fuss, knowing you got to be the martyr when she didn't agree. Besides, why did you marry her?''

''What the hell does that have to do with anything?'' He couldn't keep up with the change in topic. Nothing made sense. He felt as if he'd stepped into a conversational house of mirrors where nothing was as it seemed and even the floor beneath his feet was constantly shifting.

''You married her *because* of her stubbornness and her pride. You were attracted to her strength of character, her unwillingness to bend. You liked that she gave 100 percent and was fearless. You preached equality in marriage, singing with the choir. Yet when you married her, you expected her to be just like your mother—catering to you, making sure your needs came first.''

''You're crazy. It was never like that.''

''It was exactly like that.'' Annie May poked a finger at his chest. ''You talked the talk, but you sure weren't walking the walk. You expected Josie to cook and clean up after you, and when she wouldn't, you were left scrambling. You got mad and then you shut her out. You punished her for being exactly what she was and for everything she wasn't. There was no way for Josie to win.''

He didn't like hearing this. Annie May didn't understand. ''What about the compromises? She wouldn't even start dinner before I got home, even though she got off work first. She said it made her a slave.''

Annie May poked him again. ''Don't you find it interesting that all the compromises were about you?''

''What do you mean?''

"Did she ever ask *you* to cook for *her?* Did she ever ask you to clean her house or wash her clothes?"

He didn't like the direction this was going. "Of course not."

"Why?"

He opened his mouth, then closed it.

"Just what I thought," Annie May said triumphantly, dropping her hand back to her side. "It never occurred to you that everything was just as much your responsibility. If Josie refused to cook—which in your eyes made her a lousy wife—the compromise was either sharing the cooking or takeout. Interesting that you never offered to do it yourself. Because in your mind all the household chores were her responsibility first, and you were willing to show what a caring husband you were by agreeing to take over half the work. All the while making sure everyone knew you were doing your half, even when she should have done it all."

"It wasn't like that," he told her, even though he was getting the uncomfortable feeling that she might be right.

"Wasn't it? How come you didn't take over the cooking? Josie loved being outside. I bet she would have been as happy as a clam digging around in the yard, taking care of the lawn. Did you offer that as one of your compromises? That she do that while you did the laundry?"

When he didn't answer, she shook her head in disgust. "I figured you weren't bright enough to think of that all on your own. What about Josie's love of sports? Did you support that? Did you ever once take her up on her request that the two of you get involved in a team sport? Did you ever once play softball or tennis with her? Did you join her on a run? No. Because you wanted her home and domestic. And if she wasn't doing what you wanted, you made sure the two of you knew that she was a lousy wife. It seems to me you were a pretty lousy husband.''

He didn't need to hear this. ''All I know is that she lied to me.''

''Why wouldn't she? Would you have wanted to see her otherwise?''

He realized then that Annie May had set him up as the villain. There was no win for him. ''I'm done here,'' he said, turning and walking away.

''I'm not done with you, Delaney Michael Scott,'' she yelled after him, bringing him to a halt. Damn his parents and their training. He could no more walk away from Annie May while she was screaming at him than he could steal from the local convenience store.

''Yes, Josie lied to you and that was wrong,'' she continued. ''But do you have any idea what she's been through in the past year? Did you know that her walking wasn't a sure thing? Did you know about all the surgeries, the pain she's been through? Did you know she's not finished with it yet?''

He knew. Or he was beginning to understand. ''She told me,'' he said quietly.

''I wonder if she told you all of it. About the loneliness and the fear. About how it all had to change her on the inside as well as the outside. She's been through a trial by fire and she's a better person for having survived. What do you have to show for the last year of your life? A series of relationships with big-breasted airheads?''

He glared down at her. "You're getting real close to a line you shouldn't cross."

She stomped her foot. "I'm doing this because I love you both. Dammit, Del, can't you see what's different about her? Won't you look at all the places you failed and maybe find it in your heart to change a little? Isn't she worth it?"

No. He wanted to say no. He wanted to tell Annie May that her brutal honesty wasn't welcome in his life anymore. That he didn't want to listen to her lectures, however well-meaning.

"I can't do this right now," he said instead, moving out of the kitchen and leaving the house.

He'd come looking for Annie May, expecting a confession and some sympathy. Instead he'd been slam-dunked by a master.

His fault? She actually thought he was the one who'd been in the wrong in his marriage to Josie? That she hadn't resisted all his suggestions and acted like a child when she didn't get her way? That she hadn't been the one to walk out on nearly every fight they'd ever had? No. As far as Annie May was concerned, *he* was the bad guy. He could barely believe it.

He climbed into his truck, but instead of starting the engine, he stared unseeingly out the windshield. He wanted to dismiss Annie May's words out-of-hand. He wanted to believe with all his being that she was taking Josie's side because they were women and that's what women did. He wanted to think this was just another form of male bashing. Only he couldn't.

There was a small voice in his head murmuring that Annie May might, just might, have a point. That maybe he'd been the tiniest bit dictatorial when he and Josie had married. His old friend's crack, about him never offering to cook had made him want to protest. That wasn't his job. It was...

What? The woman's job? Because she was a woman? Josie had worked just as many hours. When she was coaching, she often worked more. So why had he assumed it was her job to take care of him? Because his mom had always taken care of him and his dad? Because it was traditional? Because he was a jerk?

He didn't like the last option so he ignored it. Instead he picked up the cell phone and called the hospital. From there he was connected to Dr. Sanders's office, where he made a consultation appointment for the following morning. Annie May might be wrong about a lot of things, but she was right about one. He didn't understand all that Josie had been through in the past year. He wanted the doctor to explain it to him in simple terms. He wanted to know the details of her surgeries and her treatment and he wanted to know what she could expect as she recovered.

And maybe he wanted to find out if what Annie May had said was true. That surviving the past year had been a trial by fire for Josie—strengthening her and changing her in ways he could never understand.

"So, you have a car," Josie said, stating the obvious. Obviously Del had a car. She was sitting in it.

Still, he seemed to understand her statement. He slanted her a quick smile and nodded. "Sometimes the truck isn't the best choice. Like now."

Meaning that she could no more have climbed up into the front seat of the cab than she could have attempted a decathlon. She rubbed her fingers against the smooth, varnished wood of the BMW's interior and told herself everything was going to be fine. Except she knew it wasn't. She hated everything about this situation.

For the past two days she'd been stuck in a hospital. Now she was finally out only to find herself in the custody of her ex-husband. Dr. Sanders had been firm. She wasn't to be on her own until she was out of the wheelchair, which could be several weeks from now. She had a list of medical restrictions and instructions including a minimum of eight hours of sleep a night, two rest periods during the day, no walking, except to shower and use the bathroom. She was to attend physical therapy sessions every day and do her stretching and exercises religiously.

Josie didn't chafe at the instructions. She knew she should have been more concerned about finding a physical therapist when she came to town and she hadn't been very good about getting enough rest. But what she really hated was the instruction that she wasn't to be on her own. And there was absolutely no driving until she was out of the chair.

Del had left her speechless when he'd volunteered to take her in. Del? The man who *still* couldn't look at her without a combination of rage and questions. He hated her. Or at the very least he was resentful of her subterfuge.

He started the engine, then pulled away from the hospital. In the spacious trunk was the hateful wheelchair. She heard it *thunk* against the side of the car as they made the turn onto the main street.

"Why are you doing this?" she asked, unable to keep the confusion and faint resentment out of her tone.

"What's the old saying? Don't look a gift horse in the mouth. It's either me, or you call your family."

She wasn't about to do that and he knew it. Her relatives had already been inconvenienced enough by her accident. Not to mention the fact that there was a part of her that didn't want to leave Beachside Bay just yet. There was Annie May, she thought, but didn't give voice to the idea. Annie May rented several small rooms at the top of an old converted Victorian house. Aside from not having room for long-term company, Annie May was in no position to carry her up and down three flights of stairs every day for her physical therapy appointment.

She sighed. She was trapped. "I appreciate your willingness to help out," she said stiffly. "But I still don't know why. Are you planning to punish me for lying to you? I've already tried to explain I didn't plan it to happen that way. I really thought you'd recognize me."

"I know."

She looked at him in surprise. He shrugged. "You're annoying as hell, Josie, but you're not a liar or deceptive. I almost understand what you were trying to do."

She doubted that, because she didn't understand it. But getting along was better than fighting. So she wasn't going to push things and she wasn't going to jump on his "annoying as hell" comment. Although she couldn't resist a murmured, "You're annoying, too."

He chuckled. "I don't doubt it for a second."

There were a few minutes of silence. The shot the nurse had given Josie before she'd left the hospital took the edge off her pain. The good news was that if she was faithful to her therapy, the doctor thought she could get rid of the constant aching completely.

"I can't believe I'm back in a wheelchair," she grumbled.

"It's your own fault."

"I know. But I still hate it." If only she hadn't been so stubborn about coming to visit Del. And if only she hadn't gotten so caught up in the past.

"If I can't get you to therapy, I'll have someone else drive you," he told her as he turned into a residential neighborhood that was familiar. "You need to get all your treatments in so you can heal."

All the quicker to get rid of her, she thought glumly. "You never answered my question. Why are you doing this?"

"I don't know," Del admitted. "Maybe because it's the right thing to do."

A feeble answer at best, she thought, wishing she was whole again. She was all mismatched pieces that might never fit together correctly. What must Del think of her? Did he despise her, or worse, pity her?

She'd handled everything badly from the beginning. She saw that now. She should have told him the truth when she'd first arrived and risked—

She blinked, then stared at the wide streets and tall trees shading the minivans and station wagons parked in the driveways.

"Where are you going?" she asked, even though she already knew the answer. Her chest tightened with the knowledge. He couldn't. He just couldn't. She wouldn't survive the experience.

"Home," he said, as if the information was of no consequence. "The Victorian house has no furniture, not to mention no kitchen. We couldn't live there. My house is a better choice.''

His house. She knew exactly what it looked like. A rambling one-story ranch with plenty of rooms, wide hallways and hardwood floors that would be easy to navigate with a wheelchair.

He turned down another street and pulled into a familiar driveway. She stared in disbelief at the gray and cream clapboard structure.

''You said you sold it,'' she whispered, hating the way her heart seemed to crack in her chest.

''No, I told you I'd send you half the profit. I decided to keep the house, so I had it appraised and calculated your share from that. I took out a second mortgage to pay you off.'' She felt more than saw him glance at her. ''Josie, you signed a quit claim deed. What did you think that was for?''

''I thought it would make it easier for you to sell.''

She'd never dreamed that he would keep the house. That he still lived here. How could he stand it, day after day facing the ghosts from their past? Then she remembered all he'd said about her and their defunct marriage. For him there weren't ghosts. Just easily dismissed memories.

She stared at the house she and Del had lived in for most of their time together. It was the place where they'd been most happy and the place where their marriage had ended. In the good times they'd made love in every room in the house. In the bad times they'd fought in the same number.

''Is this going to be a problem for you?'' he asked.

Did it matter? She didn't have anywhere else to go.

She looked at the small front porch, the clean windows, the roses bursting with life in the warm spring afternoon. She knew that the exercise room closet door stuck, that the garbage disposal could be temperamental and that when there was a bad storm, they were almost certain to lose their lights.

She could hear snippets of conversation. How they'd been thrilled with the place when they'd been newly married and house hunting. The excitement of moving in and how, surrounded by boxes and unassembled furniture, they'd stopped to make love in the center of their brand-new living room. So much laughter and so much pain. Angry words came to her along with the happy ones.

She remembered the last time she'd been inside that house. She and Del had been fighting, again. She'd started to leave. He'd told her that if she walked out on him one more time, he didn't want her to come back. In the coldest words of anger, she'd told him that her bags were already in the car. And then she'd been gone. Disappearing into the night, so sure leaving him was the right thing to do.

"Josie?"

"I'm coming back to the scene of the crime," she murmured.

"Don't think of it that way."

She looked at him, at the dark eyes and chiseled face. One corner of his mouth quirked up slightly.

"How should I think of it?" she asked.

He shrugged. "As a chance to learn how to be friends."

"Maybe," she said, but she didn't believe it. Mostly because she didn't want to be friends with Del. What she wanted was something more. But what did he want? After all this time, after forgetting her so completely and being so sure that their divorce was the right choice, why was he bothering with her?

Chapter Ten

Del carried in her small suitcase and the wheelchair he'd rented. He'd already brought over the rest of her luggage from the house. Then he returned to the car and opened the passenger door. Josie looked at him.

"Why did you take the wheelchair inside?" she asked. "I'll need it to get in."

He jerked his head toward the two steps leading up to the front door. "I don't have a ramp, and you can't maneuver over those. I'll carry you."

Before she could protest, he swept her up in his arms. When she was secure, he turned, bumping the door closed with his hip and heading for the house.

He told himself he was simply being expedient, that holding Josie like this didn't mean anything. But he couldn't help remembering all the other times he'd swept her up in his arms. His intent had usually been to get her somewhere private so they could make love. Now he was being a friend. Nothing more. Except he noticed all kinds of details. Like the fact that she felt different in his arms. Soft, rounder. She was a little heavier, though nothing he couldn't handle. But the scent of her was the same. The sweet fragrance of her skin and her hair. Her arm around his neck felt the same, too. All that was missing was her mouth pressing against his as they stumbled toward their passionate release.

No passion this time, he reminded himself. He entered the house and bumped that door closed, as well. Then he set Josie down into her wheelchair. He was startled to feel her stiffen as he put her into the seat. Instantly he dropped to one knee beside her.

"Did I hurt you?" he asked. "Is something wrong?"

She shook her head without speaking, turning her head from him. But not before he caught the gleam of tears in her eyes. Josie? Crying?

"What is it?" he asked. "Tell me."

"Nothing. I'm fine."

But she wasn't fine. He could tell from the slump of her shoulders and the way she kept swallowing as if fighting back sobs.

She reached down for the wheels of the chair, as if to move away from him. He put his hand on the frame to stop her.

"Tell me what the hell is going on," he insisted.

She whipped her head back to stare at him. He'd been right. Actual tears glittered in her eyes. She blinked and one slipped down her cheek. He reached up and caught it on the tip of his index finger. Del felt as if he'd been kicked in the gut.

"I can't do this," she said, then sniffed. "I just can't be in a wheelchair. It's too horrible."

He felt instantly helpless. He could try to imagine what Josie was going through, but he couldn't do more than empathize.

"It's only for a few weeks," he told her, taking one of her hands in his and squeezing it gently. Her fingers felt warm and familiar. He ignored the image of them touching him and instead focused on the in-progress conversation. "Your body needs time to heal. With rest and physical therapy, you'll be up and around in no time. While you're healing, you have the run of this place. I've taken up all the rugs, so you shouldn't have any trouble getting around. Just don't try any wheelies in the hallway, okay?"

His attempt at humor fell flat. She didn't even crack a smile. Instead she glared at him as if he had the intelligence of an amoeba.

"I don't understand why you're being so incredibly stupid about this," she said, practically sputtering with frustration. "I don't care about being back in a wheelchair, I care about being in a wheelchair in front of you."

With that she jerked hard on the wheels and spun away from him. She started across the living room, moving faster than he would have thought possible for someone in her weakened condition.

Slowly he rose to his feet and stared after her. His mind took off in multiple directions. Even as her confession shocked him and her pain touched him, he couldn't help noticing how well she handled the chair. Obviously, she'd spent enough time in it to become an expert. It was more proof of all she'd been through.

He swore under his breath and took off after her, grabbing her chair just before she entered the hall.

"Wait," he insisted. "We have to talk."

"Actually, we don't."

"Josie, please. It's important."

He released her and waited. Slowly, almost painfully, she turned until she faced him. She had to look up to meet his gaze. Instinctively he dropped to his knees so they were on the same level.

"I don't care that you're in a wheelchair," he told her.

"Bull. I know what happens. I've lived through it before. You're not even going to see me as a person anymore. I hate that. And I hate the control you have over me. You can grab me and turn me, taking me in any direction you want. I can't do anything but hang on for the ride."

What she was really saying was she hated the loss of control of her life.

"You're wrong," he said gently. "You being in a wheelchair means I finally get to see you as a person rather than a force of nature or a hellcat on wheels." He paused. "Although I guess technically you're more on wheels now than you were before."

Surprisingly, one corner of her mouth turned up. "Very funny," she said in a tone that indicated it was anything but.

"Oh, come on. You wanted to laugh or, at the very least, chuckle." He lightly touched the back of her hand. "You're just Josie to me. I'm still getting used to all the differences. Not just the wheelchair but the way you look, the long hair, the dresses. No one thing is that much better or worse than the other."

"It is for me."

"Okay. I accept that. But don't assume what I'm thinking, okay? Let me screw up before you yell at me."

"That won't take very long," she grumbled. "You're bound to mess up sometime in the next fifteen minutes."

"Ladies first," he quipped, then stood. "Come on. Let me show you around. I've made a few changes in the house since you were here last."

He started toward the kitchen, not sure she would follow. But eventually he heard the soft sound of rubber wheels on the hardwood floor. He stepped into the three-sided room. Where the fourth wall had been stood a center island. The old, dark cabinets had been replaced with pine. Several of the doors were etched glass instead of wood. Light granite countertops matched the color of the tile floor.

Josie wheeled her way around the area, coming to a stop in front of the six-burner stove. She raised her eyebrows as she touched the knobs.

"Either you ordered the wrong thing or you've taken up cooking in a big way."

He grinned. "Neither. A customer ordered it, then changed her mind. I needed a stove and decided to keep it for myself."

She nodded, then glanced around, taking in the recessed refrigerator and sliding cabinets concealing the small appliances.

"It's beautiful," she murmured.

"I figure it will help if I ever sell the place."

She looked at him. "All this and you really don't cook?"

"I heat microwave meals."

He took a breath to continue speaking, then

clamped his mouth shut. Telling Josie that his various girlfriends had, from time to time, prepared meals in the gourmet kitchen probably wasn't a good idea. It wasn't something she would want to hear, and he found himself not wanting to tell her.

Which led his brain down another path. Did Josie have someone special in *her* life? Someone who took care of her and worried about her? He leaned back against the island and realized it wasn't likely. At least not right now. No way would some guy let her come up here on her own.

Had there been someone before? A boyfriend or lover? He found himself torn between not liking the idea of another man with his ex-wife, which was crazy, and hoping that she hadn't had to go through her recovery alone. He knew that if he and Josie had still been together when she'd been hit by the truck, he would have been with her every moment of every day. Oddly enough, he thought she would have done the same for him.

Josie tilted her head and pointed at the upper row of cupboards. "If the dishes and glasses are up there, you're going to have to move them. I can't reach anything higher than the counter."

He hadn't thought about that. "No problem. I'll move some stuff around this afternoon and show you where I put it all later."

"Sounds good. So what other changes have there been?"

He led her around the center island to the family room, where a big-screen television took up the place of honor on the far wall.

"There's surround sound, too," he said proudly.

She laughed. "A man and his toys."

"Hey, watch it. Have you seen a movie on DVD? The difference from video is amazing. I switched a couple of years ago and don't ever want to go back. You wait. You'll get hooked, too."

She rolled her eyes, but didn't respond. Instead she followed him past the living room and down the main hall. He'd been fine with Josie sharing the house with him. At least in theory. But now, heading toward the guest room, awkwardness descended. She'd been his wife. She'd shared his bed, his life and his heart. Was she really going to sleep in the guest room, as if they'd never been more than casual friends?

"You redid the front bath," she commented.

He turned and saw she'd paused at the entrance to the small bathroom.

"It's nice," she said. "I like the tile."

He'd used a blue-and-white floral print. Not his first choice, but a bunch of it had been left over from a job. He'd gotten it at cost, so it made sense to use it.

"I, ah, I thought you'd be comfortable in the rear guest room," he said, pointing down the hall. "It's big and the bathroom has more room."

"That's fine."

She smiled but seemed to be avoiding his gaze.

Silently they moved down the hall. Del entered the guest room first. The regular bed had been stored in the garage. In its place was a rented hospital bed and a rolling table. The doctor had given him a list of supplies to have on hand. Del surveyed the walker, the television sitting on a wall shelf so it was easily visible from the bed and the floor lamp, positioned to provide nighttime reading light.

"If I forgot anything," he said turning to face her, "just let me know. I can…"

His voice trailed off as he took in the look of horror on Josie's face. Horror turned to sadness, followed by such painful resignation that Del found it hard to breathe. He couldn't remember another time when he'd known so clearly what Josie was thinking. Her pain became his pain. He wanted to scream out against the fates, protesting that it wasn't fair. That she deserved better. He wanted—

He forced himself to breathe slowly. Whatever he wanted, he couldn't do a damn thing to change her circumstances.

Josie waved at all the furniture. "You went to a lot of trouble. I appreciate that. I'll reimburse you for everything, of course."

"I don't need the money."

"Yes, well, it's the right thing to do. And you went to a lot of trouble," she repeated awkwardly. She rolled over to the walker and touched the metal frame. "At least I'm allowed to use this a few times a day. You don't need to be responsible for helping me in and out of the shower."

He had an instant image of her, wet and naked. Hardly hazardous duty. Hot desire threatened, but he pushed it away. He had no business thinking of her like that. She was his guest. She was here to heal, not provide nighttime entertainment. But he couldn't help remembering how attracted he'd been to Rose—make that Josie when she'd been pretending to be Rose.

Del shifted uneasily, unable to separate the stranger who had intrigued him from the wife he'd known before. Regardless, something about Rose/Josie had turned him on. He'd liked her feminine appearance, her smile, her body.

Apparently unaware of his inappropriate thoughts,

Josie wheeled over to the suitcases he'd set by the bed.

"You packed for me," she said.

"I doubted you could manage it for yourself. Do you want me to unpack for you as well?"

"No. I can do it. If you would please put the suitcases on the bed, I'll take care of the rest. Or at least most of it. I'll need you to hang a few things for me. After I get unpacked, I think I'll take a nap. I'm pretty tired."

He hurried to do as she requested, laying her suitcases next to each other on the hospital bed mattress. It felt odd to be doing things for Josie. She never wanted help from anyone. She was always independent.

But as he watched her maneuver the wheelchair, he had to admit that nothing would ever be the same for her again. And Annie May had been right. The past year had been a trial by fire for Josie. She wasn't the same woman she'd been before.

He had a sudden burning desire to get to know the new Josie Scott. What parts of his wife remained and what parts were different? Would she be the same when she was angry, refusing to talk and wanting to walk out? Would she make love with the same abandon and aggression or would she—

His gaze settled on her long, blond hair, then moved to her legs. She wouldn't be the same, he realized. Her physical capabilities had been diminished. He ached for her, knowing that must be the worst of it for her. Not being able to move with the freedom she'd always known. Making love would be different, but it might be better. For once he might be able to hold her as long as he wanted without her bounding away. What was it he'd said to Rose? That Josie preferred the physical to the emotional?

He groaned out loud. Josie glanced up at him. She was in the process of draping dresses across her lap so she could carry them to the closet.

"What's wrong?"

Del couldn't remember being embarrassed many times in his life, but this was one of them. Unfamiliar heat seemed to fill his body—but not the good kind of heat. He swallowed and shoved his hands into his jeans pockets.

"I'm sorry," he mumbled, barely able to look at her.

She frowned. "About what?"

"Those things I said. You know." He pulled one hand free and made a vague gesture. "When I thought you were Rose. I shouldn't have talked about you that way."

"Oh." She ducked her head. "Yes, well, I asked, didn't I?" She drew in a deep breath and looked at him. "Don't apologize. It's not necessary. If it makes you feel any better, I'll spend some time coming up with burning truths about you and I'll share them later. Then we'll be even."

She held out her dresses to him. "Would you please hang these for me? I won't be able to reach the rod."

He took her clothes and hurried to the closet. The task kept him busy for several minutes as he tried to figure out what he was supposed to say now. He'd been an idiot. Why hadn't he just kept his mouth shut? But no. He had to go spouting off.

As if his own personal humiliation wasn't enough, Annie May's words came back to haunt him. A couple of days before, she'd accused him of only pretending to compromise so that he could be the good guy while Josie took all the blame. He still didn't know if his friend had been right or not. But he was beginning to see the faults in their marriage might not have been as black-and-white as he would like.

Josie sat by the window and stared into the growing twilight. She knew that she couldn't hide in her room forever, although when the alternative was to face Del, it didn't seem like such a bad plan.

She'd managed to sleep a little after she'd unpacked. The nap had given her energy, although it had done little to brighten her spirits. She'd been prepared to have to deal with Del for a few weeks when she'd known that he'd offered to take care of her until she was walking again. She hadn't counted on having to live and breathe within the same walls that had witnessed the disintegration of their marriage.

A whisper of music teased at her memory, and she recalled a song about ghosts in the house. Fleeting remnants of memories tangling with wishes of what could have been. That's how she felt—surrounded by ghosts, some friendly, some not. If only… The magical phrase. If only things had been different.

A light knock on her closed door made her turn her chair. She smoothed her hands over the skirt of her dress, then she called out for Del to enter.

He stuck his head around the door and grinned. "Dinner has arrived," he said with a wink. "I emphasize the word *arrived* because I had no hand in the preparation. No. I take that back. I made the phone call. That should count for something. It's

Mexican and I ordered your favorites. Are you hungry?"

"Yes, thank you."

"Then come on. It's getting cold."

She forced herself to wheel toward him. He wore jeans and a white long-sleeved shirt. Nothing special. Yet he was painfully handsome, and just looking at him made her heart beat faster than was healthy.

He held the door open wide, then fell into step behind her. Self-consciousness settled on her like a cloak. She hated the feeling. She also hated that he so obviously felt sorry for her. She would rather he was angry and raging than pitying her. Everything about the circumstances that forced them back into the same house made her crazy. Worse, she couldn't imagine wanting to be anywhere else.

She went into the kitchen and found the takeout containers spread over the round pine table. A space had been made for her wheelchair. She moved toward it, but even before she got there, she knew she was going to be too low.

Del stepped behind her. "I was afraid of that," he said, then bent toward her. "If my lady would allow me?"

Before she could protest, he'd gathered her in his arms and lifted her to a regular seat.

Josie caught her breath as his strength surrounded her. He lifted her effortlessly, as if she hadn't gained twenty pounds in the past year. As if her being an invalid didn't matter.

She didn't want him to let her go. She wanted to cling to him until all her doubts disappeared and she felt whole again. Which wasn't going to happen. To cover her weakness she busied herself with her napkin.

"If you bring the walker into the kitchen before meals," she said, studying the containers of food rather than him, "I can get into a regular chair by myself."

He sat down across from her and winked. "But what if I like picking you up and carrying you around?"

"Like I'm the family cat?"

He tilted his head and studied her. "No. I don't think of you as a cat."

Before she could come up with a snappy response, he pointed to the different containers. "As promised, all your favorites. Fajitas, rice, a quesadilla and those crunchy things you like." He opened a bag and dumped chips into a bowl. "There is both hot and regular sauce. I didn't bother with margaritas because you're still on antibiotics, which means you can't drink alcohol, but I have just about everything else. What will it be? Soda, juice, water?"

"Water's fine."

Josie felt awkward and faintly foolish. She reached for a chip and nibbled on it. Del got her a glass of ice water and a beer for himself. When he was settled across from her again, he pushed the fajitas and the foil-wrapped tortillas toward her.

"Did you sleep?" he asked.

She nodded. "I'm feeling a lot better." She filled a warm tortilla with a grilled steak and vegetable combination, then spooned the hot salsa over the filling.

Del munched on a chip. "Remember when we

went to Mexico that one time," he said, taking the fajitas she'd pushed toward him.

Josie took a bite of her dinner and chewed. Mexico. She and Del had vacationed there during the first year of their marriage. "We had a good time," she said when she'd swallowed. "Well, except for that one night."

He grinned. "Hey, it wasn't the night that was so bad. It was the next morning."

She found herself smiling in return. "Too many margaritas," she admitted. "I don't think I've ever been that sick in my life."

"But we recovered quickly. Probably because we were so young."

"We had to have been younger. Older people have matured and know better than to drink that much."

They'd also made love, she thought taking a bite of rice. In those days they hadn't been able to get enough of each other. Nearly every afternoon had included a lengthy session of intimacy.

"You made me dive off that cliff," he said.

Josie wrinkled her nose. "I'd nearly forgotten. You were terrified. I was sure you were going to back out at the last minute."

"No way. You'd already jumped, so what could I do? Be a wiener dog in front of everyone in line?" He laughed. "At least I survived."

She remembered the long plunge to the water and the contrast between the heat on the top of the cliff and the cool, swirling water below. "It was great. You loved it."

His dark gaze met hers. Something almost affectionate glinted there. "Actually I *did* love it. I'm glad you talked me into it."

They shared a few more memories, then quieted to eat. Josie managed to work her way through a fair amount of food. She wasn't especially hungry but she knew she had to make sure she kept up her strength. Not eating much or well was one of the reasons she'd had the relapse in the first place.

"Josie?"

She glanced at him. He'd finished his dinner and was leaning back in his chair. To their left was the family room with its he-man television.

"What?"

He wadded up his paper napkin and tossed it onto the table. "When we were married we talked about dividing up the work around the house."

"I remember."

He shifted as if he were uncomfortable with the topic. Josie pushed away her plate. Suddenly her stomach didn't feel very good.

"I automatically took the yard work for myself," he said. "I guess because it's a more traditional male chore. Would you have liked to have done it?"

She hadn't had a clue about what he was going say, but she would never have guessed the topic to be yard work. It took her a couple of seconds to switch gears and respond to his question.

"Um, yeah, I think I would," she said slowly. "I have always enjoyed being outdoors and I like working with plants. Sure. It would have been fun. At the risk of starting trouble, that is a very strange question. Want to tell me what brought it up?"

His mouth twisted slightly. "Annie May. I spoke to her a couple of days ago. She took great delight in pointing out all my flaws. One of them was my insistence that we compromise on the household chores.

But instead of writing down all that needed to be done and deciding together how to split them, I came up with the compromise all on my own. Which, as she said, is the same as making sure it's going my way. I wanted you to agree, not to give me input.''

Josie opened her mouth, then closed it. She'd never thought about their problems in that light, but it made sense. Del *had* insisted on coming up with the compromises when there had been trouble. Some had been fine, but others she'd really hated. And when she'd protested, he'd accused her of not being willing to do her share. She'd been trapped without a way to win.

''I hadn't thought about it like that, but you could be right,'' she told him. ''We had all those fights about cooking. I always hated it. I grew up on a ranch, so I was used to hard work. I didn't mind that, but I would rather have done anything than get stuck in the kitchen.'' She leaned forward slightly. ''Not only didn't I know what I was doing, but I constantly worried about being compared to your mom. The woman is practically perfect. I always knew I was going to come up short. In my effort to avoid spending my life fetching for someone else, I probably went overboard to protect my interests.''

Del nodded slowly. ''I was crazy about the whole thing, too. Somehow cooking dinner and doing the laundry became a power play for us. We lost sight of getting the work done and focused on who had to do it and when. I never saw how expecting you to cook all the meals and be responsible for having food in the house would make you feel. I eat, too. I could have learned.''

''Or hired your mom,'' she teased.

"I don't think I could have afforded her." He shifted closer. "I'm sorry, Josie. I didn't mean to be such a jerk about it all."

His apology made her glow on the inside. After all these years she was finally finding out that maybe she hadn't been as horrible as she'd thought during their marriage. Maybe they'd both been at fault. She would have to give that concept some thought.

"I'm sorry, too," she murmured. "We kind of got stuck in a bad place and couldn't find our way out."

He nodded. "When I think back on it, I still don't know what went wrong that last year. I wanted to make it all your fault, because that made it easy for me. But it wasn't. I have blame, too."

He finished his beer and set the bottle on the table. "You're not a quitter, Josie. I've always admired that about you."

She laughed. "Thanks. As my dad used to say, 'Fitzgeralds don't give up.'"

"Then why did you give up on us?"

The difficult question—quietly spoken—caught her off guard. She searched her heart for an honest answer. "I'm not sure I gave up so much as I got tired of always losing," she admitted. "We were both young. I know I was way too young to be married. I didn't know how to be in that kind of intimate one-on-one relationship. I should have compromised more, but you're right. You were always the one coming up with the compromise. If I agreed, it felt too much like giving in. I felt as if I was bending all the time. Some days I thought I would snap. Sometimes I wanted you to bend."

Del nodded. "And here I thought I was the one doing the giving in. But I wasn't. I could make a case for it, and from the outside it looked great. But it was for show. I didn't compromise in my heart.''

She looked at the man sitting across from her. He had once been her husband, but now he was a stranger. While she appreciated the rehash of old times and the insights, she couldn't help feeling a little sad. After all, wasn't the information coming too late to do any good? If only they'd figured this out three years ago.

''I'm not proud of some of the things I did in our marriage,'' she told him. ''I was stubborn. You used to tell me it's because I was so like my dad.''

''Which you hated me saying.''

''I did. But it was true. Now, after having been through the accident and a year of recovery, I have to admit I'm glad I'm like him. It can make me difficult, but that same stubbornness and determination also got me through everything else. Without that drive and will, I might have given up.''

''I agree. Everyone has good and bad inside. You're no different from the rest of us.''

''Oh, I think my bad might be a little louder than anyone else's.''

They laughed. Then Del surprised her by stretching his hand out across the table. He held it there, palm up, obviously waiting for her to place her hand in his. Feeling self-conscious and exposed, she did as he silently requested. When his fingers grasped hers, he looked directly into her eyes.

''I want us to start over, Josie,'' he said. ''This time let's try to be friends. What do you say?''

''I'd like that.''

''Good.''

He squeezed her fingers, then released them. As she

returned her hand to her lap, she wondered what he would think if he knew the truth. That she wanted to be much more than friends. She wanted a second chance. She wanted to heal the old wounds so they could begin again. She wanted him to fall in love with her the way she was falling in love with him.

Chapter Eleven

Late one morning Josie set her book on her lap and glanced around the living room of Del's house. Her body ached from her recent physical therapy session. She was going to finish reading her chapter, then go into the kitchen and make herself lunch. After that, she wanted to take a nap. Despite finishing her course of antibiotics, she still didn't have her strength back completely. Dr. Sanders kept telling her that it would take time. It didn't help that her physical therapy sessions were grueling and left her completely drained.

The good news was, she was healing. Josie could feel the changes in her legs as her strength returned. The temptation to use the walker more than she was supposed to nearly overwhelmed her, but she resisted. This time she was going to do things right. She was going to get well enough to walk again. Maybe this time without the cane.

She gazed out the front window at the green lawn and sprawling trees. Two months ago if someone had told her she was going to be living with her ex-husband and actually liking it, she would have told that person he was crazy. Yet here she was—living with Del in the same house they'd had when they were first married. There were pockets of awkwardness, but for the most part they were getting along fine.

Every morning Del drove her to physical therapy and waited until the session was finished. He came home early from work to keep her company. They spent their evenings talking over board games or watching rented movies together. The previous Sunday they'd munched popcorn and hotdogs while watching the Los Angeles Dodgers play Atlanta in the L.A. team's first away series of the season. As he'd requested, they were becoming friends.

Josie couldn't help smiling as she thought about how careful Del was with her. He treated her as if she were a delicate creature. A few years ago she would have chafed under his concern and probably responded with sarcasm. Now she appreciated the attention. It made her feel that maybe he did care about her a little and maybe she hadn't been such a horrible wife.

Her smile faded as she remembered all the things Del had said about her when he'd thought she was Rose. She cringed at his assessment of her as a wife and a person. Unfortunately, she couldn't blame him for his opinions, nor could she point out where he'd been wrong. But the picture wasn't quite as bleak as it could have been. Because Del had admitted he had some blame in what had gone wrong, as well.

At first Josie hadn't been able to believe it. For so long she'd felt like the only flawed one. Del was so willing to compromise, offering to do his share of the chores. She'd been the one to fight his ideas. Now she could see that he'd been right when he'd said he'd been taking too much on himself. Making up his own compromises and not giving her a voice in the process was the same as getting everything his way. He'd been able to paint himself as the good guy, leaving her the role as villain.

She still wasn't sure she had completely absorbed the concept of shared responsibility in the failure of their marriage, but she was happy to make the start. Now if only she knew what to do with her growing feelings for him.

As much as she hated to admit it, Josie knew she was in trouble. Being around Del was an odd combination of old and new. Unfortunately, it was the best of both worlds. She liked the changes in him, while all the things she'd loved about him before still existed. How was she supposed to resist that? How was she supposed to keep her heart safe? While he was being very kind and obviously cared about her, caring wasn't love. They had affection but not passion. And while she wanted to believe that a happily-ever-after ending was possible, her daddy hadn't raised a fool. Wishing and reality could be worlds apart. She would have to—

The slam of a car door cut through her thoughts. Josie returned her attention to the window, wondering if Del had forgotten something at home. The thought of him walking through the front door sent her heart into hyperspeed. She clutched the arms of her wheelchair and ordered herself not to grin like an idiot.

But the person who came into view wasn't Del. Instead it was a young woman, maybe twenty-four or twenty-five. She was tall, lean and gorgeous, with flame-red hair that tumbled down her back. Jeans clung to impossibly long legs. A cropped long-sleeved shirt dipped just low enough to expose the top curves of a showgirl-size chest. She moved with the grace of a dancer…or an athlete.

For several seconds Josie could only stare as the woman approached the house. Her brain offered explanations for her presence. She was selling something. She was lost. She had the wrong house. She was a neighbor.

Then she pulled a key out of the front pocket of her jeans and Josie *knew* the truth. She was Del's girlfriend. Someone close enough to warrant having access to his house when he wasn't home. Someone…

The key turned in the lock. Josie gasped and put her hands on the wheels, but there was no time to run and nowhere to hide. Instead she was forced to stay where she was, right in the middle of Del's living room, and wait to confront someone who was too much like the woman she, Josie, used to be.

The woman stepped into the foyer and glanced around. When her gaze settled on Josie, she started visibly. Josie didn't have a clue as to what the visitor was thinking. She was too busy dealing with her own thoughts.

Del's girlfriend was everything Josie would never be again. Graceful, straight, unbroken. She could walk or run or dance without effort. She could move her legs and arms, wear a bikini without worrying about scars. She could make love anywhere, in any position. She was physically perfect.

The woman blinked first. "Who the hell are you?"

Her outrage, her slightly pouty lower lip, all eased Josie's tension. For some reason she suddenly found the situation slightly amusing. She was in a wheelchair for heaven's sake. How much of a threat could she be? Yet the woman was staring at her as if she were the devil himself.

In that second Josie made a decision. She knew it was both wrong and childish, but she couldn't help herself. So she gave her guest her best smile.

"I'm Josie Scott. Del's wife. And you are?"

The woman's gaze narrowed. If her eyes had been a laser beam, Josie would now be a puddle of steaming goo. "I'm Jasmine, Del's girlfriend. And I know for a fact that he's divorced. Which makes you his *ex*-wife."

Don't do it, Josie ordered herself. She had no right to interfere in Del's personal life. Maybe this woman was someone important to him.

She mulled over that thought and found she didn't believe it. He'd been spending all his free time at home. Unless Miss Congeniality had been out of the country for the past month, they weren't getting along all that well. Besides, Del had kissed her, Josie. He wasn't the kind of man to do that while he was involved with someone else. Although there *was* the matter of the key.

She told herself to be nice.

She didn't listen.

"I'll admit to being his ex," she murmured softly. "But haven't you heard that possession is nine-tenths of the law. That would mean I live here now and you don't."

Jasmine's full mouth twisted. "I don't believe you."

"You don't have to. Ask Del yourself. He'll tell you that I'm staying with him indefinitely."

Jasmine took a step back. "No way. He wouldn't want someone like you when he could have me. Del isn't into pity and why else would he want a cripple."

With that she turned on her heel and stalked out of the house. Josie tried to tell herself that the ultimate victory had been hers, that she'd driven the younger, pretty predator out of her territory. But the words didn't offer any comfort. Not when she was forced to accept the truth.

Jasmine was right. Del wouldn't be interested in Josie. She was too different, and even if her body had been as perfect as it'd been before, he hadn't liked her personality all that much. His actions were two part kindness and one part guilt. Nothing more. Despite her fantasies to the contrary, he wasn't falling for her.

Unfortunately, there was no way to stop herself from falling for him.

Annie May arrived a little after twelve. She brought with her a large bag from a local burger place, along with a six-pack of Josie's favorite soda.

"I heard," the older woman said when she'd helped Josie into a regular chair at the table and had put out their food. Humor glinted in Annie May's eyes. "Jasmine flew into that office like her pants were on fire. I don't usually spend much time there, so I might have missed it all, but Del had called a staff meeting. We'd just finished and most of the guys were long gone, but I was still chatting with Jan about her kids.''

Josie wasn't sure she wanted to hear what her friend had to say, but she couldn't help the curiosity welling up inside of her.

"She was upset?"

Annie May bit into her burger and chewed. When she'd swallowed, she raised eyebrows. "*Upset* doesn't quite cover it. She was out for blood. She stormed into his office and slammed the door so hard the windows rattled." Annie May grinned. "It was almost like having the old you back again."

"That's hardly a compliment," Josie muttered. She didn't want to be reminded of her past. Nor could she believe Del would get involved with another woman who had a temper. "Has Jasmine always been volatile?"

"Not that I knew about." Annie May dragged a couple of French fries through a puddle of ketchup. "But he's been slowing things down with her for a few months now. I don't think she's been real happy at the thought of the relationship ending. I guess this was the final straw."

"So what happened?"

Annie May chuckled. "They were going at each other like two tomcats. She was screaming and he was trying to calm her down." She sighed. "Don't men know they only make things worse when they act reasonable while we're all upset?"

"I guess not."

The older woman shrugged. "Anyway, Jasmine demanded to know who you were. I couldn't hear Del's answer, but I'm guessing he told her the truth. She let out a shriek they probably heard in China. Then she began stomping around, demanding that he get you out of his house. He raised his voice enough for us to hear him tell her it was *his* house, and he would do as he pleased. Then he told her it was over between him and her and asked for his key back. She got really ugly, calling him names and saying you—''

For the first time since she'd started the story, Annie May hesitated. Josie knew what that meant. Jasmine had talked about her condition, saying unkind things about the wheelchair and maybe Josie's appearance.

''I can guess,'' she said, turning her burger over in her hands but unable to eat.

''Well, the good news is Del took his key back and showed her the door. She was still spitting fire as she stomped to her car. Then he got all embarrassed, knowing we'd heard just about everything they'd said, so he slammed his door. That's when I decided to bring you lunch.''

''I hope Del ended his relationship with Jasmine because he wanted to and not because of me,'' she said, feeling slightly guilty for what she'd said to the redhead.

''Liar,'' Annie May announced. ''You don't want that man of yours thinking about anyone but you.''

Trust Annie May to cut to the heart of the matter, Josie thought. ''Maybe, but I'm also a realist.''

''What does that mean?''

She sighed, then set down her burger. ''Look at me. I'll never be the woman I was. My life is a mess and Del isn't going to want to be a part of that. He's only taking care of me now because he feels sorry for me. He's never going to want me—not while there are women like Jasmine around. Why would he settle for someone who will never be completely whole again? I can't do any of the things I used to do. I can't run or ride or play sports. I can't even do my job. No school is going to want a cripple for a PE teacher.''

Annie May took another bite and chewed it slowly. Josie fought against the burning in her eyes. She wasn't about to give in to tears. She had already done that once this month.

Her friend wiped her hands on a paper napkin, then took a drink of her soda. ''I thought you had some attitude going for you,'' she said. ''I was impressed by the way you handled Jasmine. Whatever you said put her in her place. But I see I was wrong. So this is where I tell you that people who sit on the pity pot look real silly after a time and they get a permanent red mark on their butt. That's not your style.''

Annie May's words stung. ''That's not fair. I'm not feeling sorry for myself, I'm stating the reality of the situation. Don't you dare tell me that I'm giving up. I've worked damn hard this past year. Harder than I've ever worked for anything. Until you've lived through what I have, don't you dare judge me. You can still do just about everything you want to. You don't understand and you never will, so don't you ever presume to judge me.''

Red eyebrows raised slightly. ''Well, you go girl. I'd wondered if there was still some of the old spirit left in that body of yours. I'm glad there is.''

Her reaction didn't make sense. ''What's your point?''

Annie May leaned toward her. ''I don't want you getting lost in your pain, Josie. You're too strong for that. Yes, your situation is pretty horrible. It's not fair and it's never going to be fair. But everyone has to overcome something. Your thing is just a little tougher than most. But you're improving. You're doing more than surviving, you're learning to live again. Don't let go of that. You're healing and you have people who care about you. That's more than a lot of folks can say.''

Josie didn't want to admit it but she knew her friend was right. ''I see your point,'' she said slowly. ''But I still hate my physical limitations.''

''Hate all you want. Just don't feel sorry for yourself. You still have a lot going for you. You don't have to worry about money.''

Josie nodded. Her settlement from the company that owned the truck that hit her had been more than enough to take care of her for the rest of her life. Her medical expenses were covered, as well.

''You might not look the same, but you're still pretty.''

''I'm not complaining about my face.''

''I know. It's your body. You can't do what you used to. Hell, I can't either, but that's a byproduct of growing old. When I get crabby I remind myself about the alternative, which is being dead.'' She grinned. ''Not my first choice. As for your life, so you can't be the coach you were before. You still love sports. Can't you find some way to be a part of them? What about the kids who have physical limitations? Who teaches them to play on teams? Who shows them what their bodies are capable of and how to be a winner from a wheelchair?''

Josie blinked. ''You mean like a special education PE teacher?''

''I don't know. That's your field of expertise, not

mine. I'm just saying that if you want to still be involved with kids and make a difference, there's nothing stopping you. You've got your brain. Use it.''

Josie considered the possibility. She'd assumed that because she couldn't go back to her old job, teaching was no longer available to her. But maybe she'd been too quick to give up. Maybe there were alternatives.

''Which leaves only one thing,'' Annie May said, her brown eyes intense and focused. ''That fool man of yours.''

Josie swallowed. She didn't want to talk about this because it would mean admitting her secret desire. Something she'd barely been willing to think in the darkest corners of her mind. Yet if she didn't say the words aloud, they couldn't be real.

''I want him back,'' she whispered, not looking at her friend. ''I want a second chance at a marriage. I still love him and I want him to love me back.''

''So where's the problem?''

Josie shook her head. ''He doesn't love me. At times I think he doesn't even *like* me very much. Our past is too much to get over. Besides, he's been involved with other women.''

''You were divorced, honey. What did you expect?''

That Del would pine for her. That his life would crumble when she left. Not that she could tell Annie May that.

''Jasmine wasn't about being in love,'' her friend said. ''She was about being lonely. Yes, Del has dated and been involved, but he hasn't been in love with anyone. You're the one who used to have the key to his heart. The lock might be rusty, but I know it hasn't changed. Find that key and use it.''

"I'm afraid," Josie admitted.

"You can't win if you don't even try."

"What if I lose?"

"At least you'll have the truth. And you'll be able to look yourself in the eye, knowing you gave 100 percent."

She would also have a broken heart. She realized now that she'd never stopped loving her husband. She'd locked her feelings away and refused to look at them. It took a life-threatening accident to bring them back to light. If she tried to win back Del and lost, she would be destroyed. If she didn't try, she was going to be destroyed. There didn't seem to be many options.

"Del, your mom is on line two."

Jan's voice came through the intercom. Del bit back a curse as he dropped into his seat and reached for the receiver.

Ever since Jasmine had exploded into his office, he'd been trying to get home to check on Josie. He didn't know what she'd thought of his ex-girlfriend showing up the way she had, but he doubted she'd been happy. He couldn't call to check on her because she didn't pick up his phone line, and events had conspired to keep him stuck in his office for the past several hours.

First there had been the theft of some equipment at one of the job sites. Then a zoning commissioner had dropped by to talk to Del about a planned development on the bluffs overlooking the ocean. There had been phone calls from customers, and a minor dispute between employees. Finally, when he was about to walk out the door and head home, his mother called.

He pushed the button on the intercom. "Thanks, Jan," he told his secretary/receptionist, then punched the flashing button for line two. "Hey, Mom. How's it going?"

"Fine, Del. Your father and I are in Kentucky and we absolutely love it here. The grass is the most extraordinary color, and the horses—" she sighed "—they're stunning. I'm making noises about wanting to retire here but your father refuses to listen."

Despite his need to get home, he couldn't help smiling as he listened to his mother's voice. "Dad would miss the water."

"I know. He keeps reminding me. And I tell him that we could have our very own pond, but he's not impressed. So what are you up to these days? How's work?"

Del's grandfather had started the family construction firm. Del's father had taken it over, then had passed the business on to Del. For most of the years of their marriage, Catherine Scott had not only taken care of the house, her husband and her son, but she'd also helped out in the office several mornings a week.

"Business is good." He hesitated. "Someone bought the old Miller place. We're doing the remodeling job."

"Really?" Delight brightened his mother's voice. "I'm so happy. I adore that old house. Frankly, it deserves new owners. Those last people just let it sit for so long. Tell me about the new owners. Are they putting the master on the third floor?"

"Yup. In fact I got approval on my plans earlier this week. We'll be starting the framing Monday."

Catherine laughed. "Good for you. I always did like that design. The master suite is going to be spectacular. So tell me about the family that bought the house. Do they have many children? That house cries out for the sound of laughter. What do they think of the neighborhood? Are they—"

"Mom," he said, cutting her off. "One or two questions at a time, please."

"Oh, all right. So, spill the beans."

He leaned back in his leather chair. What was he going to say? How could he explain what was going on in his life? He didn't expect his parents to either approve or disapprove, but he doubted either of them would be silent.

"Josie bought the house. She's back in town."

There was a moment of silence, then the sound of his mother exhaling slowly. "Josie? After all this time?"

He couldn't tell from the tone of her voice if she approved or disapproved. "I was surprised, too."

"Are you two getting along? If you're doing the remodeling, you must see quite a bit of her."

He'd come this far, he thought wryly. He might as well get it all out in the open. "She's staying at my house temporarily."

Then, before his mother could respond, he filled her in on Josie's accident and her subsequent recovery. He explained how she'd collapsed and was spending a few weeks in a wheelchair. Finally he outlined his offer to take care of her during that time, which meant her living at his house.

"I see," his mother said slowly. "Josie in a wheelchair. I can't begin to imagine what that must be like for her. She was always such an athletic girl. Running, playing sports. And so pretty. Is her face really completely different?''

''I didn't recognize her for a while,'' he admitted. ''She's still attractive, but she doesn't look like herself.''

''That must be odd.''

''I'm getting used to it.''

''Del, I...'' His mother cleared her throat. ''I don't know if I should say this or not, but I'm going to. I love you very much and I always liked Josie. When you told me you were getting married, I thought you were both a little young, but your father and I hoped you would mature together.'' She paused.

Del braced himself for what was coming. Obviously, he and Josie hadn't matured, at least not in a way that allowed them to keep their marriage together. He knew his mom was going to warn him against getting involved with Josie again. Probably very sensible advice but for some reason, he didn't want to hear it.

''I've always felt terribly guilty for my part in breaking up your marriage.''

He stared at the phone. ''What? Mom, you're crazy. You didn't do anything to hurt my relationship with Josie.''

Catherine Scott sighed. ''Not directly, perhaps, but I did have a minor role. You see, I know how Josie felt about me. We got along very well, but she was intimidated by the way I had always taken care of you. She couldn't compete with that and I doubt she wanted to. To be honest, I didn't want her to, either. What if she'd done a better job? Still, she had to feel inadequate. She didn't cook or bake and she'd never really learned to run a household. To make matters worse, you had an expectation that your wife would be like me, at least in the homemaking department. I was too old-fashioned that way.''

Del hadn't thought there were any more surprises left regarding the situation between himself and Josie, but he'd been wrong.

''Mom, I—''

''You don't have to say anything,'' she told him, cutting him off. ''I can't change what I did while you were growing up. I love you and your father. Taking care of you both was my way of showing that love. So except for how it affected your marriage, I don't have any regrets. But Josie was so different. I think she wanted to try, but she didn't know how. I could have helped more, but I didn't. I was sad as I watched your relationship falter, and I didn't know how to make it better.''

''That wasn't your responsibility.''

''I know, but every mother wants to protect her children from their own mistakes. Unfortunately, children need to learn on their own.''

He wasn't sure what to make of all his mother had told him. There had been more forces at work while he and Josie had been married then he'd realized. The question was, what did he do with the information now?

After Annie May left, Josie tried to take a nap, but her brain wouldn't shut down enough for her to sleep. Dozens of thoughts and ideas circled through her mind. She tried to absorb all that had happened.

Of course she was upset about Jasmine's visit, but she told herself she was really dumb if she thought that Del had been a monk for the three years they'd been divorced. Obviously he'd dated. But as Annie May had pointed out—he hadn't fallen in love. There had been no serious relationships, which was good for her.

She also thought about what her friend had said about her, Josie, still having the key to Del's heart. She wanted that to be true, but she wasn't sure. She was slowly coming to believe that she wasn't the only one at fault in the marriage. Unfortunately, if they were both to blame, it would also take both of them to fix the problems. And she wasn't sure Del would want to participate in that. She wasn't sure about anything where he was concerned.

"A grown-up would come right out and ask," she told herself, speaking aloud into the quiet of the room. Unfortunately, she wasn't feeling especially mature at this moment. Maybe an alternative would be to test the waters in more tentative ways, so she could feel safer during the process.

She closed her eyes and found herself remembering all the fights they had about her cooking…or rather her refusal to cook. For Del, coming home to a freshly cooked meal had meant a lot. But she'd resisted right up to the end. She would cook, but only when he was there to help.

She turned on her side as she remembered that his favorite was lasagna. Catherine had shared a recipe with her once. It was supposed to be one that he really liked and, according to her then mother-in-law, relatively easy. She'd tucked the paper into a cookbook. Josie sat up. She would bet money that cookbook was sitting right above the small desk in the kitchen and that the recipe was still inside. She could make that for Del tonight, as a surprise.

Then she glanced down at her legs. She wasn't allowed to drive. Nor was a wheelchair easy to maneuver in a grocery store.

"Delivery," she said with a grin.

She would make up a shopping list and call in the order. Then she would get started with her surprise dinner.

Chapter Twelve

Three more crises had followed his mother's phone call, which meant Del didn't pull into his driveway until after five that afternoon. He sat in his truck and wondered what he was supposed to say to Josie. Bad enough that Jasmine came by the house, but worse that Josie had been there to witness it. Plus, Jasmine had had a key in her possession. What would Josie think about that?

He shook his head. He knew exactly what she would think—what anyone would think. That he and Jasmine were close enough to be physically intimate and coming and going freely in each other's homes. Which might have been true at one time, but wasn't anymore.

Guilt made him not want to go inside. He tried reminding himself that he and Josie had been divorced for three years and what he did in his free time wasn't her business. He almost believed it, too. But not quite. Something had happened when he'd brought Josie home with him. Not so much an emotional connection between them as an unspoken agreement about responsibility. He hated that Jasmine might have said some pretty cruel things to Josie. He wanted to apologize for them but wasn't sure if mentioning them would make the situation better or worse.

After a couple of minutes he reminded himself that acting like a coward got nothing accomplished. He stepped out of the truck cab and headed for the front door. As he used his key to let himself in, he half expected something to come flying at his head. Josie wasn't violent by nature but she could be a little aggressive when provoked.

But she wasn't there to greet him. In fact the house was surprisingly quiet. There weren't even any lights on anywhere. His chest tightened with the realization that something might be wrong. Or she could have left him.

"Josie?" he called anxiously.

"Oh, hi. I'm back in the kitchen. But I have to warn you to be careful where you step."

She didn't sound mad. In fact, he couldn't place the tone of her voice. Not angry, not even upset. If anything she sounded rueful. Which didn't make sense.

He headed for the back of the house and rounded the corner to head into the kitchen. He came to a stop as abruptly as if he'd run into a wall. His mouth dropped open as he stared at the disaster that was his state-of-the-art kitchen.

"Josie?"

She looked up at him and shrugged her shoulders. "I want to tell you that it looks worse than it is, but it's pretty bad. The thing is, I didn't do it on purpose."

She sat in the center of the kitchen floor. Her light-blue dress had several red stains on the front, and there were a couple of dark smudges on her cheek. Behind her two pots sat half on, half off the stove. The scent of something burning filled the air. A jar of spice had tipped onto the counter and trailed down to the floor. A heavy stock pot lay next to her. Water pooled around her, while limp lasagna noodles oozed toward him in a slow-moving river. Her wheelchair looked as if it had been in a food fight. It leaned precariously against the pantry cupboard.

She made a vague gesture toward the mess. "Sorry."

He couldn't believe it. "What were you doing?"

She gave him a sheepish smile. "Cooking. Or at least trying to. I remembered that lasagna was your favorite. I had this recipe your mom gave me years ago, so I dug it out and decided to make it. Except the counters and stove are too high and I was afraid to be on my feet too much. Things got out of control really fast. I stood a couple of times, then I lost my balance and slipped, which explains the noodles on the floor. That's about when you walked in. So would you please help me up?"

Nothing she said made sense. She'd been cooking? For him? Why?

"Where'd you find the recipe? You couldn't have been carrying one around with you all this time."

"I'd tucked it into one of the cookbooks." She

pointed to an open book on the counter. "It was still there. Um, Del? I'd really like to get off the floor."

"What? Oh, sure. Sorry."

He moved toward her, then bent down to collect her in his arms. As he gathered her close, her hair brushed against his cheek. The soft sweep of waves smelled delightfully floral. Her body was warm and curvy, fitting perfectly against his. Suddenly he didn't want to carry her just to a kitchen chair. Instead he wanted to make the journey to his bedroom at the end of the hall. A bedroom she'd once shared with him. He wanted to place her on the mattress and carefully undress her. Then he wanted to make love with her, touching her everywhere, kissing her, tasting her, bringing her pleasure until she was lost to everything but the feel of him against her. Until she was spent, yet still begging for more.

"Del?"

The sound of his name jerked him back to reality. He realized he was crouched on the floor, cradling Josie against himself.

"Not that this isn't comfy," she teased. "But I think I'll do better in my chair."

"Let me clean it up first," he said, rising to his feet.

He moved her to the kitchen table and got her settled. Then he retrieved her wheelchair and began to wipe off the various spills. His body heated with excitement, which he tried to ignore. He didn't dare look at her or face her. Not only would she be able to read the truth in his eyes—she would see it physically manifested in other parts of him.

Could she make love, he wondered as he wiped the metal frame clean, then brushed off the seat. Were there limitations because of her accident? Would the act itself hurt her? He thought about pressing himself on top of her and didn't know if that would be too much for her healing body. There was no polite way to ask, nor was it any of his business.

Except he found himself wanting it to be. He wanted to know if she'd been thinking about him in the same way. Had she been as caught up in the possibilities?

Behind him, he heard her clear her throat.

"I've been an idiot," she said quietly. "I moved in here without giving the situation a second thought. I didn't realize I was cramping your style."

Arousal or not, that made him turn to face her. "What are you talking about?"

She held up her hands in front of her, palms up. "Isn't it obvious? You know that Jasmine stopped by today. I should have realized you were involved with someone." She dropped her chin slightly and stared at the floor. "I didn't mean to be thoughtless. I'm sorry."

He pushed the wheelchair out of the way and crossed to the kitchen table. When he was in front of her, he reached into his right-front pocket and pulled out a single key.

"You're not cramping my style," he said, setting the key on the table. "I was seeing Jasmine, but things have been winding down for a while. After she came here, she dropped into the office." He remembered the younger woman's outrage and cruelty. "Let's just say we decided it would better if we didn't see each other anymore."

Josie touched the key. "I don't think it was that simple. I feel bad for messing up your life."

He dropped to a crouch in front of her. "Do you really think that's what happened? If she'd been that important to me I wouldn't have invited you to stay here. You know me well enough to trust my word on that."

She raised her gaze until it met his. He saw questions in her blue eyes. Questions and a desire to believe him.

"You sure?" she asked.

"I swear."

"Okay. Then I'll believe you."

"Thanks." He lightly touched the back of her left hand. "I'm sorry she stopped by. It never occurred to me she would show up here or I would have gotten my key back before. I know you weren't prepared for her visit."

Josie gave him a smile. "Oh, let's just say we startled each other. While it wasn't a genuine cat fight, we each showed a little fang and claw."

"Did you kick her butt?" His tone was teasing.

She shrugged. "I tried. I think the altercation was a draw."

He wanted to ask more. He wanted to know if she was really okay or if Jasmine had hurt her feelings. But he didn't know what words to use without making it into a bigger deal than it was. He also didn't want to embarrass Josie.

"Want me to get Annie May to beat her up for you?" he asked.

Josie rewarded his joke with a chuckle. "Oh, sure. Send an old woman to do your dirty work."

"I don't know who else to ask. My mom's out of town." Which reminded him.

He straightened, then moved to the chair next to

hers. "I spoke to my mom today," he said. "I mentioned you'd bought the old Miller place and were having it remodeled."

"Really?" Josie looked wary, and Del couldn't blame her. "Did you happen to tell her that I was staying with you?"

He nodded.

She swallowed. "Great. I can't even begin to imagine what she said."

"Actually she surprised me by saying she was sorry about how she'd interfered with our marriage."

"What?" Josie stared at him as if he'd suddenly sprouted wings. "She apologized? This would be your mother, Catherine the perfect?"

"That's her. She said she knew that she did you a disservice by spoiling me while I was growing up. She said it gave me unrealistic expectations. Not that I agree with her, of course."

Josie dismissed him with a wave. "You wouldn't. You live to be served."

"Well, I don't *live* for it, but I don't mind it when it happens." He let the humor fade from his voice. "She also said she felt guilty about how she'd secretly been glad that you weren't as domestic as her. She didn't want to have to compete."

Josie stared at him. "She really said all that?"

"Yes. She liked you a lot. I guess she's sorry things didn't work out."

She looked as if she was about to say something, then didn't. Del wanted to hear her say, "Me, too," as if she was sorry the marriage had ended. Which didn't make sense. They'd been divorced for three years. Their relationship was finished. Which didn't explain why he desperately wanted to kiss her. His most recent attempt had ended with the revelation of her true identity. He wondered what would happen if he tried it again.

"Thanks for telling me about your mom," she said. "And I'm sorry about the mess in the kitchen."

"Not a problem. I appreciate your attempt to make me lasagna."

She chuckled. "I guess I should have started my cooking career with something more simple. So what do you want for takeout tonight? I was kind of thinking of Italian, if I haven't scared you off that."

"Sounds great."

"I was so sure I could do this," Josie said, later that evening when they'd finished their dinner. "Apparently lasagna is something I should wait to tackle when I'm more upright. What do you think?"

He thought she was beautiful, but didn't think he should share that. She might not understand how he meant it. Or maybe she would know exactly what was on his mind. What would she say if she knew how much he wanted her? Would she smile at him the way she used to when she read the desire in his eyes, or would she politely, gently refuse him?

"Del?"

"Huh?"

She leaned forward, resting her elbows on the kitchen table. They'd spent the better part of an hour cleaning up the mess from her failed cooking project, then had ordered in pasta from a nearby restaurant. Now the remains of their meal lay in front of them.

"I was asking you if you would like me to try cooking lasagna again when I'm back on my feet."

Her question had so little to do with what he was

thinking that he had a hard time responding. "Oh, yeah. Sure. That would be great."

She stared at him, then drew back in her chair. She pressed her lips together. "I'm sorry. That was really presumptuous of me." Her voice sounded small, as if she had been hurt by something he'd said. Color crept up her face. "You're probably thinking you'll never get rid of me. But you will. I promise. Just as soon as I can walk, I'll be out of here and you can have your life back."

Her discomfort, not to mention the rush of words, got his attention. He realized that she was embarrassed, assuming he hadn't responded because he wanted her gone. Which couldn't be further from the truth. He also realized that three years ago he would have taken her words the wrong way. He wouldn't have seen the defensive posture or the blush. Instead he would have gone defensive himself, figuring she was trying to be the one to leave, rather than the one left. That it was all about her, rather than them.

"Josie, I'm enjoying having you stay here," he told her. "I'm not looking forward to having you gone, so let's not talk about it. As for you cooking me lasagna, I would like that very much."

Her eyes brightened. "Really?"

"Sure. After the way I've been catering to you, you're going to owe me some home-cooked meals. I intend to collect every single one of them."

"Deal," she said with a grin. "However, I should probably start with simple stuff. Remember the time I tried to make you a birthday cake? It was so crooked. I thought I could fix it by applying a little extra frosting, but it didn't help."

"What I remember is the color. You made it that weird blue-green."

"It was teal," she said, sounding amused and faintly defensive. "I wanted a baking color, but something a little masculine."

"Cakes are, by definition, *not* masculine. And who ever heard of teal frosting?"

"I couldn't find it anywhere so I had to make it myself. With food coloring. It took a long time to get the blend right."

"Did you ever think about the fact that if it wasn't available for purchase that there might be a reason?"

Her mature response was to stick her tongue out at him. "It wasn't all that bad."

He pressed his hands on the table and rose to his feet. "Actually it was, and I have proof."

He walked into the family room, to the cabinet against the far left wall. On the bottom shelf were a couple of photo albums. He picked them up and set them on the coffee table in front of the sofa. Then he returned to the eating area and carried Josie the few feet to the sofa.

"This is torture," she complained as he set her on a cushion. "I'd forgotten you'd taken pictures. It's cruel to remind me of my lone baking failure." She glanced at him and giggled. "Don't you dare mention it's the only cake I ever tried to make."

"Would I say that?" he asked as he settled next to her. "Let's see if I can find the proof here somewhere."

He set the first photo album in front of them. Flipping the pages forward, he let them fall open randomly. As he glanced down, his breath caught in his throat. He hadn't found the birthday cake pictures.

Instead the two exposed pages contained photos from their first Christmas morning together.

Del's throat tightened as he stared at the moments in time, frozen in vivid color. Josie ripping open packages, her flannel nightshirt tails riding up her leg to her butt. Her short blond hair was mussed, her face makeup-free and bright with anticipation. Several more pictures showed her holding up a white see-through nightie. In the last picture on the pages, she'd unbuttoned her plaid nightshirt and was holding it open enough for him to see the hollow between her breasts. Her mouth formed an exaggerated, sexy pout, her eyes danced with amusement.

Josie, so lean and carefree. Moving easily, knowing that her body would do whatever she asked. Her face... He leaned forward and studied the familiar features. Features that had little in common with the woman sitting next to him. Even knowing they were the same person, he had trouble reconciling the past with the present.

"I look so different," she said quietly, reaching out and rubbing one of the pictures. "Younger. I can't decide if I was pretty or not then. I think I was."

"You were," he said and risked looking at her. "Pretty and full of life."

Sadness softened her expression. There weren't any tears or hints of self-pity, yet he knew this had to be difficult for her.

"We don't have to look at these if you don't want to," he said.

"I think I would like a little trip down memory lane. If you don't mind."

He shook his head and turned the page. More Christmas pictures, these taken at his folk's house. He and Josie had gone there for dinner. There was a photo of the table, perfectly decorated in red and green with a huge pine-and-red-rose centerpiece.

"Your mom sure knew how to set a table," Josie said, pointing to the gleaming crystal and silver.

But Del was paying more attention to her. Sitting this close, and on her right, he could see the tiny scars under her chin and by her ear. He'd never noticed them before, but now he recognized the permanent marks of her surgery. Her skin was smooth and tight, her mouth and eyes as they had always been. But the rest of her was so very different.

"You're beautiful now," he said without thinking.

She turned to look at him. Doubt darkened her eyes. "You think so?"

"Yes. You were pretty before, but now you're beautiful. Not just your face, but your hair, too." He touched a blond curl. "I like it long."

She blushed slightly and turned her attention back to the album. "Yes, well, I did wear it short before, didn't I?"

"Too short."

She squinted at the pictures. "I'd have to agree with you." She sighed. "Although I do miss that body."

"I don't. I like this one."

She grimaced. "That's because you haven't seen it. Trust me, it's not attractive. Not only are there parts that don't want to work right, there are also some pretty angry looking scars. Not to mention the twenty pounds I've gained."

"I like the curves."

"Really?" She glanced at him out of the corner of

her eye. "I do have cleavage for the first time in my life. That's kind of nice."

He thought about asking to see it, but figured that was way out of line. Instead he continued flipping the pages of the album, documenting their history in single moments. There were vacation trips and more holidays. When they were finished, he reached for the second book, then paused.

"You up to this?" he asked.

She touched the lace-edged cover. In the center of the album was an oval containing a picture of them standing together on their wedding day. Josie wore a white lace wedding gown, fitted and sleeveless. Del was in a dark tux.

"I can stand it if you can," she murmured.

He could. He opened to the first page. One of their wedding invitations had been tucked into the binding. Josie pulled it out and opened the flap of the envelope. There was a picture on the front—of her and Del together in a park. He was carrying her piggyback and they were both laughing at the camera. It was late fall, but a warm day because they were both in shorts and T-shirts. They looked happy and impossibly young.

Without thinking, he slipped an arm around her shoulders. The second he realized what he'd done, he wondered if he should pull away or leave it in place. Fortunately, Josie snuggled close and leaned her head on his shoulder. When she sighed, he felt her soft breath on his neck.

"Turn the page," she said when she'd replaced the invitation. "I want to see the rest of it."

He did as she requested, flipping through their rehearsal—a casual affair with Josie carrying a bouquet of ribbons and bows from her wedding shower—to the crowd that gathered for the ceremony itself.

"There's your dad," he said, pointing to a tall man looking uncomfortable in his tux.

She nodded. He remembered that all of her family had come out for the wedding. A.J. and David, her oldest brother, had been ushers. Her sisters had been bridesmaids with young Blair and Brent acting as ring bearer and flower girl. Until Del had seen all the Fitzgeralds together, he hadn't realized how large her family was, or how small his appeared by comparison.

There were pictures of the ceremony and the reception, and a few pages from their honeymoon in Hawaii. In the back was an envelope. At first Del didn't realize what was inside, then he started to laugh. He reached for it, but Josie grabbed it first.

"I don't think so," she said, straightening and holding it away from him.

But when she pulled out the pictures inside, she didn't prevent him from looking over her shoulder.

There were ten photos in all, taken with an instant camera. Josie was in their honeymoon hotel room, posing for him. She was nearly naked in all of them, vamping like a model, being coy in one picture and bold in another.

"So strong," she whispered, rubbing her finger along the length of her muscled leg in one picture. "I felt like I could take on the world. Now I feel weak and boneless. As if I could collapse and fade away at any moment."

He took the pictures from her and shoved them back in the envelope. "You're not weak, Josie. Anything but. You couldn't have gone through what you have without being strong. It took guts and courage to face the pain and the months of physical therapy. You're the strongest, most determined person I know. I'm sorry for all the suffering you went through, but I can't do anything but admire the person you've become.''

Josie wanted to believe him. Most of the time she would have, but not now. Not after seeing all those damn pictures. She'd forgotten how perfect she'd been. The suppleness of her movements, the lean strength, the grace. Then she'd raced and danced and dashed. Today she lurched and hobbled and stumbled. So many memories of something that could never be again.

"Don't," he said, cupping her face in his hands. "Don't you dare start disappearing into feeling sorry for yourself. I won't let you. You've lived through a trial of fire and you've come out a better person on the inside. Don't wish that away.''

His hands felt warm and powerful. She wanted to ask him to never let go.

"Can't I have both? My new-and-improved personality along with my old body?''

"I don't think it works that way.'' His dark eyes were intense with emotion and something she might have thought was…desire? No. That was crazy. Del couldn't want her. Not now. Not like this.

"I was thinner back then,'' she said, both as a complaint and a warning.

"Yeah, and I was always worried about being impaled on a hipbone or done in by an elbow. Now you're curvy in all the right places.''

She swallowed. Could she believe him? She desperately wanted to but she wasn't sure. "Don't say things just to be kind,'' she said, shifting away from him.

But Del didn't let her go. Instead he moved closer and bent down to kiss her. The touch of his mouth against hers was almost painful in its tenderness. So light, so perfect. Possession, desire and a promise all blended in the one brief brush of skin on skin.

What was he doing? When he pulled away, she tried to speak and couldn't. Her throat felt too tight. Her heart was pounding so fast she was afraid it was going to wear itself out.

''Del?''

''If you're asking me what's going on, I don't have a clue. All I know is that I want you.'' He touched his fingers to her mouth, preventing her from saying anything. ''It's not pity. It's real. I want you.'' He brushed his lips against her cheek. ''I want you in my bed. I want to make love with you.''

She didn't know what to think, what to feel. Was this really happening? Could she believe him? How could she know he wasn't just feeling sorry for her?

He swore under his breath. ''I can see the doubts in your eyes,'' he said and reached for her hand. Then he placed it flat against his groin.

She felt the hard ridge of his desire. Something hot and hungry flared to life inside of her. He really did want her. Broken or not, different or not. He wanted her.

And she loved him.

''Say yes,'' he requested. ''Please say yes.''

She couldn't have said anything else. He was the man she'd always dreamed of.

''Yes,'' she whispered. ''As long as we can do it right now.''

Chapter Thirteen

Before Josie knew what was happening, Del swept her up in his arms. Since she'd moved in with him, he'd carried her many times. Mostly from her wheelchair to the sofa, or from her wheelchair to bed. She told herself she should be used to the feel of his arms around her, supporting her. But this time was different. This time she would swear she could feel the heat and desire filling him. This time his hands seemed especially tender where they touched her. This time he murmured her name, then brushed a kiss across her forehead. His actions almost made her grateful that she couldn't walk like a normal person.

"My room?" he asked, then chuckled low in his throat. "Make that *our* room?"

She hesitated, then nodded. Their room. She hadn't allowed herself to go back into that section of the house. Every time she'd been tempted, she'd re-

minded herself that she was his guest and she owed
him his privacy. But she'd wondered if it looked different, if he'd changed the furniture or the bedspread.

He walked toward the wooden double doors. The
left one stood ajar. He turned sideways to slip inside,
flipping on the light switch as he went, then crossed
to the bed and set her on the mattress.

Josie looked around, taking in what was the same
and what was different. The furniture—the big king-
size bed, the nightstands and the dresser—were all
familiar, but the bedspread was new, as were the shut-
ters at the windows. She remembered drapes. He'd
pulled up the carpet and had replaced it with a hardwood floor covered with several small scatter rugs.
The fireplace in the corner was now brick instead of
river rock. The space was a disquieting combination
of old and new. She felt she was living through a
dream where reality kept changing and shifting until
she couldn't maintain her balance.

Del sat next to her and took her hand in his. "Are
you all right? Have you changed your mind?"

She shook her head, then realized he wouldn't
know what she was denying. "I haven't changed my
mind. It's just…strange to be here."

"Would you rather make love in the guest room?"

Those two words, *make love,* made her shiver as
desire flared up inside of her. Would the guest room
be better? She decided it didn't matter where they
actually became intimate. There were ghosts in every
part of this house. And not just the ones from their
marriage. Even though she knew it was stupid, she
couldn't help wondering about the women he'd been
with since she'd left. How many had there been? How
beautiful, how young, how undamaged?

Unexpectedly her eyes began to burn, as if she was close to crying.

Del touched her chin, forcing her to look at him. "What are you thinking?"

She sighed. There wasn't much point in avoiding the truth. He was going to see it for himself in just a few minutes.

"I saw Jasmine," she whispered. "There have been others, too, I'm sure. Plus there are the pictures we found. The ones from our honeymoon."

He frowned. "Josie, I have no idea what you're talking about."

If she'd been able to, she would have slid off the bed and started pacing. As it was, all she could do was half turn away from him and hunch her shoulders forward.

"My body," she said flatly. "It's different. Not just the loss of muscle or the weight gain. I have scars. Some are old, but others are still red and thick. I've lost a lot of flexibility. I don't bend the same. I can't get in all those crazy positions anymore. Everything is going to be different. I just wanted you to know that."

Speaking the words made her ache inside. She didn't like being different and she hated having to tell him about it. She wanted to turn back the clock and be the person she'd been before. Except she liked the emotional lessons she'd learned in the past year. If only she could have gotten the latter without having to be hit by a truck.

He touched her shoulder, urging her to face him again. When she didn't move, he spoke anyway.

"Do you think I care about scars or the fact that we can't do it like professional gymnasts?"

There was a long pause, and she realized he expected her to answer. Slowly she shifted until she could look at him. He stared at her—all intensity and fire.

"I don't know if you do care," she admitted. "That's what makes this difficult. Plus, no one has seen me. I mean no one other than a medical professional."

He smiled. "I promise I won't run screaming from the room. As for the rest of it, Josie, *you* matter. All of you. No part is any more important than another, except for your brain. Because that's who you are. It's about your insides way more than your outsides. Please believe that."

"I want to."

"Then take a chance. I meant what I said before. I think you're beautiful. Scars and all. As for having to make love differently, I'm not frightened of that. Slow and seductive isn't a punishment. Besides—" he reached up and tucked her hair behind her ear "—we can think of it as a second first time. For us it will be as if we've never made love before. How many couples get that kind of second chance?"

He was saying all the right things. She desperately wanted to make love with him, but there was so much fear.

"Trust me," he whispered as he pulled her close and pressed his mouth to hers.

She melted into the kiss. His mouth was that impossible combination of firm and soft. Just the way she remembered, she thought, as heat began to steal through her. His lips moved against hers, rediscovering her, letting her rediscover him. She liked that he went slow, brushing against her over and over, teasing with his tongue at the corner of her mouth, but not dipping inside. Not yet.

Instinctively she raised her hands to his shoulders. From there she slid one into his hair and rubbed the other up and down his back. He was exactly as she remembered—hard and unyielding. Thick muscles shifting as she touched them. He cupped the back of her head, as if he was afraid she would bolt. She wanted to tell him that she wasn't going anywhere, but she didn't want to break the kiss long enough for her to speak.

He dropped one hand to her shoulder. As his strong fingers began kneading away her tenseness, his tongue swept across the seam of her mouth. She instantly parted for him—opening to let him inside.

Even as they began the intimate dance she recalled so clearly, her body surrendered to desire. Her breasts swelled, becoming exquisitely sensitive. Low in her belly, a shiver trickled through her. It moved down, between her thighs, making her ache with longing. She could feel herself readying for him. Her woman's place remembered the feel of him inside of her—how he'd always had the ability to bring her the most perfect release.

But this was more than just needing ease from sexual tension, she thought, as his tongue teased hers and made her moan low in her throat. She desperately wanted the connection with Del. She wanted to be in his arms, held close. She wanted to feel skin on skin. She wanted tenderness as well as sex.

The need made her feel vulnerable, which made her uncomfortable. But not wanting to deal with it didn't make it go away. So she concentrated on his warm breath and the heaviness of his hand on her waist.

Del shifted slightly, as if he were going to lie on the bed. Without thinking, she moved to straddle him. Her on top was a position they'd always favored. She half turned in her seat and raised her left leg to slid over his. Instantly pain ripped through her, making her gasp aloud and collapse on the bed.

"Josie?" Del bent over her, stroking her face. "What happened? What hurt you?"

She couldn't speak. It was as if someone had set fire to her bones…and not in a good way. Pain seared her, making it impossible to talk. She could barely breathe. Humiliation joined the agony, making her want to scream her frustration. It wasn't fair. Please, God, why couldn't it be fair?

"Josie?"

"I'm fine," she managed, breathing out the words more than speaking them. "Just give me a second."

She rubbed her thigh in an effort to ease the sensation. Del's hand pressed over hers.

"Does rubbing help?" he asked.

She nodded.

He pushed her fingers away and began to move in a slow, deep circle. He was stronger than her and he had the advantage of being able to sit up and press into the movement. At first his ministrations only made it worse, but gradually the tension eased and she was able to move again.

"Thanks," she said as she sat up. She was careful not to look at him. Embarrassment flooded her. If she'd been able, she would have left his room and then his house, without once looking back.

But she couldn't leave. At least not yet. She could only sit there and search for words to explain.

"I told you I couldn't do the things I'd done before."

She knew the statement sounded like an accusation. As if it was Del's fault.

"I understand. So what went wrong?"

She laced her fingers together. "I tried to swing my leg over yours. I thought I'd straddle you. But I can't lift my leg in that direction."

"You hurt yourself. Is it temporary or do you think we should get you to the doctor?"

"I'm fine."

Just leave me alone. Except she couldn't say that part because she didn't want to be alone. She wanted to be with Del, but only as her old self.

"Do you still want to make love, or did that kill the mood?"

She couldn't believe he'd asked. She turned to glare at him. "I know you can't want me anymore. Not like this."

He raised his eyebrows. "I don't recall saying what I wanted. I asked about you. How do you feel?"

"Why does that matter?"

"Because you're half this team." He leaned close and kissed her. "What I learned from what just happened is that we have to be really careful. I'm happy to do that. What I need to know is if you still want this or if you're too sore."

Words failed her. He still wanted to do it? Now? After she'd demonstrated how different it was going to be?

"But we might have to use pillows to support my hips," she said uneasily. "And I won't be able to wrap my legs around you or anything."

"Wow. That's pretty terrible. I'm completely grossed out."

As he spoke, he angled his head so that he could kiss the side of her neck. She shivered at the delicate contact.

"You're not being serious."

"You haven't given me a reason to be. Do you like this?"

He took her ear lobe between his teeth and gently bit down. Another shiver rippled through her, this one erasing the last of the pain. Suddenly she could feel the dampness between her thighs and the ache in her breasts. Tension spiraled through her, making her blood run hotter and faster.

She pulled away so that she could see his face. "Are you sure?"

He smiled then. That "I'm so damn male" smile men got when they knew they were about to get lucky. "Oh, yeah."

She couldn't help smiling, as well. "Promise you won't be grossed out too much."

"You have my word."

He shifted so he could slide one arm behind her back and the other under her legs, then he moved her so that she was lying on the mattress.

"Just relax," he told her as he stretched out next to her. "Let me do all the work. Your only job is going to be giving me instructions."

She tried to ignore a flutter of nerves in her stomach. "I like doing that."

"I know. So have at it. Tell me if you want more or less or harder or faster. Whatever seems right at the time."

As he finished speaking, he bent over and kissed

her. At the same time, he reached for the front button of her dress and unfastened it.

Josie told herself to concentrate on the feel of his mouth against hers, on the way their tongues instinctively moved together in a pattern they'd established years before. She tried to focus on how right it felt to be with him, to be next to him, in bed with him. But she couldn't. All she could think about was the row of buttons giving way beneath his questing fingers and how he was going to pull her dress open at any second and then he would be able to see a lot of her body and it wasn't very pretty and he was going to want to call the whole thing off and he wouldn't know how so she was going to have to do it but she really, really didn't want to because—

One hand settled on her breast. The contact startled her, making her gasp against his mouth. But the quick exhalation came more from how good his palm and fingers felt than from horror. In fact there was less and less horror as he began to move against her curves. The lace of her bra was barely any barrier at all.

She knew she was fuller than she'd been the last time they'd made love. He slowly discovered all her fullness, then gently rubbed her nipple between his thumb and forefinger. The attention was exquisite, making her arch slightly against him.

She wanted to raise her hips and part her legs, but she didn't. She was careful to keep her movements small so she wouldn't set off any more pain explosions.

As his fingers teased her breast, his tongue teased her mouth. The combinations of contact made her want to whimper. Everything he was doing felt so very good. She'd been skin-starved for so long. The thought of another man doing this to her was impossible to imagine, but with Del she suddenly knew she would be safe.

"Josie," he whispered against her mouth as his hand began to slip lower. Fingertips drifted across her belly, circling down to that most secret place between her thighs.

It was only then that she realized he'd unfastened her dress to the hem. Darn those buttons, anyway. They made her too accessible.

Not that she was going to complain, she thought dreamily as his fingers rubbed against her. Through the thin layer of her panties, he found that one place designed to make her scream with delight. She parted her legs to give him more room and forced herself not to arch into his caress.

He moved in a steady rhythm. Around and over, making her sigh and shudder and reach for that perfect moment of release. Past and present merged. How many times had he touched her like this before? How many ways had he pleasured her? It didn't matter if he used his fingers or his tongue, if he was inside of her or not, he could always push her to the edge, then catch her as she fell.

"I want to do more," he breathed against her mouth. "I want to crouch between your legs and kiss you there. I want to use my tongue to make you scream."

His words made her dampen even more. Her breathing increased and she found she was clinging to him as if she was in danger of being swept away.

"Next time," he promised. "We're going to be

more traditional tonight. Just to get you comfortable with me.''

She managed to distract herself from the growing pressure so that she could open her eyes and look directly at him. Passion tightened his face. She gave a slight smile.

''I'm feeling very comfortable,'' she murmured.

''Are you sure?''

''Oh, yes. Very sure. And very comfortable.''

His fingers continued to move as they spoke. Around and over. Gently faster, then slower. Teasing, always teasing.

''Am I doing it right?'' he asked. ''Could I do anything differently?''

A sudden heat flared on her cheeks. She wasn't usually embarrassed about sex, but this was different.

''Um, well, we could take off my panties.''

She forced the word out, her need larger than her shyness. Because if her panties were removed Del would continue to touch her, but without the scrap of silk between them. He would continue to stroke her most sensitive place but he would also push his fingers inside her. Just the thought of that was nearly enough to send her flying.

''Done,'' he said, and dropped a quick kiss on her mouth.

He moved so that he could shift to his knees. It was only then that Josie realized her fatal mistake. Now he could see her legs.

''Del, don't,'' she said, reaching down to cover herself with the edges of her dress.

His gaze met hers. ''Don't what?'' he asked. ''Touch you?''

He demonstrated the action by sweeping a single finger between her legs. Despite herself, she moaned.

"Don't what?" he repeated, then lowered himself so that he could kiss the top of her left thigh. "Don't think you're lovely and wonderful? Don't imagine myself deep inside of you? Don't remember how it felt to take you and be taken by you?"

Each word fell on her, branding her, making her recall how it had been between them. Her breathing quickened. When he swept his hands up the length of her legs, she found if she didn't think about it too much, she actually didn't mind. She felt the ridges of her assortment of scars and knew he felt them, too. But he didn't look at them. Instead he kept his gaze locked with hers.

Slowly he reached forward and pulled down her panties. Then he returned to her side and drew her into a sitting position. When she'd shrugged out of her dress, he unfastened her bra and slid it down her arms. Finally he settled her back on the bed and stretched out beside her. His mouth returned to hers while his fingers resumed their delicate torture.

But this time was so much better. This time there wasn't anything between them, not fabric, not even air. He brushed against her swollen wetness and dipped into her waiting heat. Over and over he thrust into her, mimicking the act of love to follow. His mouth trailed down her throat, then moved lower until he took one nipple between his lips. His tongue flicked against her. That combined with the gentle movements of his fingers was too much for her. She clutched the bedspread and prepared herself for flight.

Higher and faster and lighter and over and around. How he touched her. He knew when to concentrate on that single spot and when to push a finger inside. The pace increased. He returned his mouth to hers, kissing her deeply until she couldn't hold back anymore. It had been so very long, and she'd so missed making love with Del.

That was her last conscious thought as the pleasure shuddered through her. Her body trembled with release. She called out his name over and over as she soared into the perfection of the release. And when she was finally still, she found herself cradled in his arms.

Seconds passed, then minutes, where she struggled to catch her breath. When she was finally still, he brushed her hair away from her face.

"I want you," he murmured.

"Yes," she told him. "Please, be inside of me."

He rose to his feet and quickly stripped off his clothes. Shirt, shoes, socks, jeans, briefs. Until he was naked.

Josie looked at him, at the breadth of his shoulders and the way dark hair lightly covered his chest. Time had honed his muscles. He was still beautiful, especially that most male part of him. He was also very aroused. The proof of his desire made her feel safe and wanted.

He moved to rejoin her on the bed, but she raised her hand to hold him off.

"Protection," she said. "I'm not on anything and parts of me are still completely intact."

"No problem." He opened the nightstand and pulled out a sealed box of condoms. After opening the container, he removed one, then returned to her side.

They kissed deeply. Although she'd already had

her pleasure once, Josie wanted more. She needed to feel Del inside of her, filling her the way he used to. Tension radiated from him—more proof that he was as ready.

"It's time," she murmured against his mouth.

"Are you sure?"

"Absolutely. Just go slowly. I don't know how much I'm going to bend."

His gaze turned serious. "Tell me if anything hurts. I don't mind stopping." He hesitated, then grinned. "Okay, I'll mind a little but I'll still do it."

She nodded, then parted her legs as far as she could. Del applied his protection and positioned himself between her legs. He stopped long enough to grab pillows and place them under her knees, then he gently moved his hips forward.

She felt him enter her. Slowly, so very slowly, filling her until she knew she couldn't stand anything more of this extraordinary pleasure. She stretched around him and felt her body collecting for the first pulse of her release.

When he was all the way inside, he paused. "Are you all right?"

She nodded. There was a slight tugging in her hips, but nothing she couldn't ignore. She desperately wanted to tilt her pelvis to invite him in further. However she knew the folly of that move. Spending the next fifteen minutes screaming in pain would be a mood breaker.

Instead she let him do all the work. She tightened around him with each thrust but otherwise was still. Del moved slowly but steadily, filling her over and over again. Tension increased with each penetration until she couldn't hold back anymore. The first shuddering release swept through her.

He groaned with her climax. His gaze sought hers.

"I can feel that," he gasped in amazement, his features tight with passion. Then he swore and bent low to kiss her.

She found herself caught up in a chain reaction. With each thrust, she lost a bit more of herself to the release. The slow rhythm was making her crazy in the best way possible. She never wanted it to stop. Over and over she shuddered until she was exhausted and content. Finally he gave one last, deep thrust and was still. She was so in tune with him that she felt the pulsing rush of his own competition. They stared at each other in that moment of perfect communication, two truly united as one.

Del pulled the covers over Josie and himself, then drew her into his arms.

"You okay?" he asked.

She leaned her head against his shoulder and sighed. "That's the fifth time you've asked me. I'm going to stop saying yes in a second."

"I want to make sure I didn't hurt you."

"Del, you redefined my role in the universe, but you didn't hurt me." She snuggled closer and closed her eyes. "Thank you. That was spectacular."

"I liked it, too."

She shoved at his arm without opening her eyes. "Don't you dare pretend it wasn't amazing."

He smoothed the hair from her face and smiled into the night. "*Amazing* works for me."

Amazing and a bunch of other words like *incredible* or *unbelievable*. Sex with Josie had always been great, but tonight was one of the only times he re-membered making love with her. There'd been a closeness, a connection he didn't recall from their past. Being inside of her had changed everything. Or maybe it had just exposed the truth.

He was falling in love with her.

Del shifted so he could raise his free arm and slide his hand under his head. Josie's slow breathing indi-cated that she was already falling asleep. He'd always appreciated that she wasn't one of those women who liked to talk after sex. That hadn't changed.

But many other things had, he thought, remember-ing her concerns about him looking at her scars. She'd been scared and vulnerable. Two very unnatural states for his ex-wife. But she'd faced down her fears, which was 100 percent Josie. He was having trouble rec-onciling the person she'd been, with the person she'd become.

The impatience was gone, as was her anger, he thought, although given what she'd been through in the past year it made sense that she would be more intense. Instead Josie had gentled. He felt different, as well. Maybe they'd used the time apart to grow up. Had they changed enough?

He stroked her hair and heard her murmur his name. If he was falling in love with her, what was going to happen now? He hadn't allowed himself to think about the future, but here it was—looming.

He thought about all the women he'd been with after the divorce. He'd enjoyed them but he'd never loved anyone but Josie. She'd claimed his heart eight years ago, and he'd never bothered to get it back.

"I like you holding me," she whispered in the dark, sounding sleepy. "You feel good."

"You, too."

"Was I..." Her voice trailed off. "Were you surprised?"

At first he thought she was asking about them making love. Then he realized she meant the scars. Had they shocked him? He thought about the lines on her legs. Some were pale, others were still red and thick. There were scars on her stomach, her arms and a thin one down the side of her left breast. Three years ago she'd been physically perfect. Today she was everything he wanted.

"I wasn't surprised that it was still good between us," he told her. "You always were a hot babe."

She giggled. "That's not what I meant."

"I know." He turned and kissed her forehead. "The scars only matter to me because they meant you were in pain once. Otherwise, I don't even see them."

"But we had to do it differently. I couldn't get in any weird positions."

"I don't care about that. I like doing it the old-fashioned way. Making love doesn't have to be a sporting event every time."

She sighed. "We used to do it standing up, Del. I can't do that anymore."

He pulled her tighter against her. "When you were gone, I missed the sound of your laughter and the way you smelled. I missed making love, but when I thought about that, I never once imagined us doing it against the door. I swear."

"You promise?"

"Yeah."

"Okay." She sighed and was still.

Del enjoyed the feel of her curves next to him. What exactly were they talking about, he wondered.

It seemed to him they were skirting around the issue of their marriage. They were living in the same house and they'd just become lovers. Did that mean they were going to give it another try? He wanted to believe it might work, but he wasn't sure. Josie had lived her life to be independent, and he wasn't interested in a relationship in which he wasn't needed. So where exactly did that leave them?

Chapter Fourteen

Del cooked steaks on a grill on the stove while Josie prepared the salad. He'd found a butcher-block cart that was the perfect height for her to use from her wheelchair. As she sliced cucumber, he checked on the meat.

Their conversation was as easy as their movements. Josie told herself not to read too much into the situation, but she couldn't help hoping that Del thought things were going as well as she did. They'd been lovers now for three days...and nights. They'd been sleeping together in the same bed, reaching for each other in the darkness. Yesterday he'd come home for lunch, but they'd never exactly gotten to a meal. Instead he'd carried her into the bedroom and had made love with her. He treated her with affection, respect and tenderness, and she couldn't help hoping that love was just around the corner. But she couldn't be sure.

When he was at work, she sat alone berating herself for not having the courage to tell him how she felt. It should be so easy to say the words, to admit her feelings. He'd loved her once—couldn't he learn to do it again? Or had there been too much time and damage?

"The kitchen cabinets are finished," he was saying, speaking of the progress on her remodeling project. "I'll be hanging them next week. In the meantime I'm getting started on the bathroom cabinets."

"I can't wait to see them." She reached for a tomato. "How's work coming on the master suite?"

"Great. We're a couple of days ahead of schedule. Everything should be done in three weeks. Your new house will be all ready for you."

His words should have made her happy, but they didn't. She didn't like thinking about moving out of Del's home. She liked being here, with him. But she didn't know how *he* felt. Was he enjoying their time together or did he want his old life back? When she was finally mobile was he going to give her a kiss goodbye and simply tell her thanks for the good time?

The thought made her chest ache. She hated that it took being in a wheelchair to make Del keep her around. That meant their living arrangement was all about convenience and not a matter of the heart. She'd been faithful about her physical therapy appointments and her exercises. She'd been resting, as well. Now all that was paying off. She was stronger than she'd been since the accident. When she stood in the shower, she no longer swayed like a drunken sailor. She knew that at her next doctor's appointment she was going to get the all-clear to start using her cane again. Which meant there was no reason to stay here. She would have to move out and then what would happen?

She desperately wanted to ask but she was so afraid of his answer. She didn't want to know that this had all been a game for him. A way to relive the past. She didn't want to know that she no longer mattered.

She finished the salads and carried them to the table. Del turned over the steaks.

"What are you going to do with the house?" he asked, his back to her as he watched the grill. "Are you going to keep it or sell it?"

The unexpected question made her tense. "I don't know," she admitted. "I haven't thought that far ahead."

"You seem to be moving around better. I'm sure Dr. Sanders is going to be pleased when she sees you the first part of next week."

It was as if Del could read her mind, she thought in panic. Was he making conversation or trying to get rid of her?

"I've been doing everything she told me," she said weakly. "Doctors tend to like that in a patient."

Del flipped the steaks again, then turned to face her. He wore his usual jeans and flannel shirt. The casual clothes emphasized his strength. When he folded his arms over his chest, the shoulder seams strained.

"I've liked having you here, Josie. We're doing well together."

"I agree." She swallowed. She didn't know where the conversation was headed and it made her nervous.

"I wish you'd contacted me when you'd first been hurt. I would have been there."

"Why?" she asked bluntly. "We were divorced.

We hadn't seen each other in two years. What difference would my accident have made?''

"We'd been divorced for three years when you showed up here."

"That was different. I wanted closure."

Something shifted in his eyes, but she couldn't tell what he was thinking.

"Did you find it?" he asked.

She shrugged, still unable to tell him that she'd thought of him in that last moment when she'd believed she was going to die. "I wanted to know what had gone wrong between us. I guess I needed to tie up some loose ends." She smiled. "You provided me with a detailed list of my faults, that's for sure. I now have a very clear picture of everything I did wrong."

He winced. "I'm sorry for all the stuff I said when I thought you were Rose. I was a jerk."

"You were honest. It wasn't fun to hear, but I needed the information. I like to think that I've changed since then."

"In some ways. But your basic spirit and determination are alive and well. I'm glad."

They gazed at each other. Something passed between them but Josie didn't have a clue as to what it was. Her heart was too engaged, she thought. She wasn't able to read his signals because she didn't want to know anything bad.

He returned his attention to the steaks. "Annie May said you'd been talking about returning to teaching."

"It's crossed my mind. Not only do I have the training, I miss it."

"She said something about special-needs kids." He glanced at her over his shoulder. "Is that what you want or is it all you think you're capable of?"

She couldn't help laughing. "Gee, Del, I thought I was the one who asked the blunt questions in this relationship."

"Hey, I learned from a master. So which is it?"

She considered her answer before speaking. "I suppose in my heart I know that I could go back to what I was doing before. There might have to be some physical adjustments, but I would still be a good coach. But the idea of working with kids who have physical limitations is appealing to me. I've been through the surgeries, I felt what it's like to try to walk when every cell of my body is screaming in pain. I've lived with the despair and dying hope. While I would love to take a basketball team to the state championship, I think I would do a lot more good helping a child have fun from a wheelchair."

He put down his tongs, crossed the room and kissed her on the mouth.

"What was that for?" she asked as he returned to the grill.

"No reason."

Maybe not, but the action had left her all tingly inside. She had to catch her breath before she could speak again. "I've spoken to my sister, Katie. She's the physical therapist."

"I remember Katie."

"She said that there are lots of opportunities for what I'm talking about."

Del felt himself being ripped in two. On the one hand he liked everything Josie was saying. Her words illustrated the changes in her and made him hope that they had a future together. On the other hand he didn't know if she planned to pursue her new career here or somewhere else. Was she in his house because she wanted to be or because it was convenient? Was their newfound intimacy just a quick trip into the past, or had he managed to touch her heart?

The simplest way to find out would be to ask, but he didn't want to hear the answer if it was no.

In the past few weeks he'd come full circle with Josie. At first he'd been attracted to a stranger named Rose. Then he'd been furious to find out she was his ex-wife. Now he was discovering new things about her that made him know he'd been crazy to think he would ever forget her or stop loving her. He wanted them to have a second chance, but this time he wanted it to work.

He turned the meat again. He was cooking them on a low flame to make sure they stayed tender. Josie had already prepared baked potatoes which were wrapped in foil and waiting on the table.

"We both made a lot of mistakes when we were married," he said, not looking at her. "For a long time I thought all the fault was yours, but it wasn't. I screwed up, too. At least half of the blame is mine."

"Relationships are about sharing," she teased.

He glanced at her. Fading sunlight caught her blond hair, bringing out faint traces of gold. Her skin glowed, her smile was tender. Just looking at her made his heart ache.

"You're tough," he said. "You're stubborn. You're not a quitter. I know I asked this before, but I still want to know why you quit on us."

The laughter left her eyes and she sighed. "I don't know, Del. I've asked myself that same question. I guess a lot of it is that I liked to be a winner and I could never win with you. All my life my dad had pounded the concept of being right, of winning, into me. Nothing else mattered to him. I didn't know how to compromise, I didn't know how to say, 'We were both wrong.' Or if I'd said it, I didn't know how to believe it. I literally had to get hit by a truck before I figured out that winning isn't everything. That I don't always have to be right.'' Her mouth turned up at the corners. "I know I look really bright but occasionally I'm a slow learner.''

"It took Annie May reading me the riot act to figure out that I hadn't exactly been the perfect husband. So I guess we're even.''

She smoothed her skirt over her lap. "I've spent the past year figuring out my strengths and weaknesses. I've had to learn to depend on people. I couldn't do it all myself. That's been a hard and ugly lesson and I still forget it from time to time.'' She paused. "I'm sorry I was so immature when we were married. I'm sorry I didn't know how to talk things out.''

"I'm sorry I was a jerk who expected you to cater to his every whim.''

She chuckled. "I'm many things, but I'm sure not like Catherine. I never will be.''

"I never wanted you to be my mom.'' When she raised her eyebrows, he held up his hands in a gesture of surrender. "Okay, maybe I did want you to take care of me the same way, but I know now that was unrealistic. Besides, you were amazing in very nonmaternal ways.''

Her gaze narrowed. "You're talking about sex, aren't you?''

"Oh, yeah. You were always hot, Josie. You still are.''

He expected her to laugh, or at least smile, but she didn't. Sadness darkened her eyes.

"I can't be like that anymore, Del. That part of my life is over. If you're waiting for it to reappear, it's not going to happen."

He heard the pain in her voice, and it frustrated him. "Dammit, Josie, you're talking about doing it up against the wall again. Why are you fixated on that?"

"Because it's lost to me. I'll never be that woman again."

"Who says I want her back?"

"You just did when you talked about me being hot. Which doesn't make any sense because when you thought I was Rose you said our sex life before was lousy."

He turned off the grill, then walked over to crouch in front of her. Her eyes were huge and her mouth straight. He could see he'd hurt her.

"Chemistry," he said touching her cheek with his fingers. "We have great chemistry. We're both spontaneous. It's about attitude, not location or position. As for what I said when I let my lips flap without my brain engaged, I'm sorry."

She jerked free of his touch and turned her head away. "Being sorry doesn't change the truth. I thought I was at least good in bed when we were married, but I w-wasn't."

His throat tightened as her voice cracked. Del knew he'd done serious damage and he didn't know how to fix it. Except with the truth.

"I wanted more, Josie," he said quietly. "The wild crazy sex was fun, but I needed a connection that was more than physical. I wanted to be able to hold my wife in my arms and stroke her hair. I wanted her to make love with me, then hug me and never let go. I wanted tenderness, not just getting off. I wanted what we have now.''

She turned back to him. Tears filled her eyes. ''I didn't know how to be tender. I didn't know it was important. No one had ever been that way with me. I thought you would want it fun and different and exciting.''

''That part was really good, but it wasn't enough.''

A single tear rolled down her cheek. She brushed it away impatiently. ''But now when I can give you tender, I can't give you the other part. I like being in your arms. I like you stroking my hair, and when we hug, I don't want to let go. But the rest of it is gone forever.'' More tears spilled down her cheek. ''So you're destined to be disappointed with me.''

He hadn't known it was possible to feel this much pain inside and keep on breathing. There weren't any more words, he realized. He could tell her it didn't matter but she wouldn't believe him. So he was going to have to show her it was still possible.

''You're wrong,'' he announced and rose to his feet.

He quickly pulled the salads from the table and pushed the place settings and potatoes to the side. Then he returned to her and picked her up. She shrieked.

''What are you doing?''

''Proving my point. We can talk and talk, but it won't make any difference. You'll never believe me. You might have learned tender, but you sure didn't forget stubborn.''

He set her on the kitchen table. Before she could

figure out what he was going to do, he reached under her dress and pulled down her panties. She yelped in protest. He ignored her. Seconds later she was sitting bare butt on the table. He tugged off her panties, then dragged over two chairs. He placed one foot on each chair so she had plenty of support. Only then did he move between her parted thighs.

He was pleased to see that her tears were gone. She looked ready to spit fire.

"Don't for a moment think you can coerce me into having sex with you now. Let go of me right this instant. You're nothing but an animal."

He placed her hands on his shoulders and nestled against her. "Point one," he said as he brushed his mouth against hers. "You're determined to believe we can never have wild, spontaneous not-in-bed sex again. This is a demonstration to prove you wrong. Point two, stop protesting. You could have stopped me at any second and you didn't. If you don't want to make love right now, simply say so and I'll stop. Point three—"

She reached around to put her hand on the back of his head and brought him close for her kiss. "Point three," she said before claiming his mouth with hers, "shut up."

Del had thought that Josie might resist his graphic proof that they could be as inventive as they'd been before…with a little bit more innovation, but he'd been wrong. She pressed herself against him with an eagerness that had him hard in about thirty seconds. Desire swept him up in a passionate tide from which there was no escape. Apparently Josie was equally affected, for even as her lips clung to his and her tongue invaded his mouth, she reached for the belt of his jeans.

He reached down to help her. They fumbled with the fastenings and freed him. His instinct was to plunge inside of her, but he forced himself to hold back. Instead he reached beneath her dress to test her readiness. After all, just a couple of minutes before she'd been near tears.

He slid his fingers along her thigh and made his way to the center of her being. There he encountered slick, welcoming, damp heat. She moaned when he made contact. As he moved a finger inside of her, he used his thumb to locate her most sensitive spot. He'd barely brushed against her when she shuddered. He felt the rippling response of her release around his finger. The feel was so erotic, he nearly lost it himself right there.

"Del, please," she moaned against his mouth.

He pulled up her skirt and prepared to thrust inside of her. At the last second he swore and pulled away.

"What?" she called after him as he turned and hurried from the room.

"Protection," he yelled, heading for the bedroom. Once there, he grabbed one from the open drawer and jogged back to the kitchen.

Josie sat where he'd left her, but there had been a couple of changes. She unbuttoned her dress and shrugged out of it so the fabric pooled at her waist. She'd also taken off her bra. Her breasts were full, her nipples hard. Sexual desire tightened her expression, but there was also a smile tugging at her mouth.

"What's so funny?" he asked as he ripped open the condom's packaging.

"Us. We're in the kitchen, doing it on the table.

Neither of us is completely undressed. In fact all you've done is unzip your jeans."

"Yeah, well, we can get fancy next time." He shoved his jeans down to his thighs and quickly applied the protection. "I thought you liked that we were spontaneous."

"I do. Very much."

She started to say something else, but he thrust inside of her, and instead of words, she screamed. He felt her instant release. She clung to him, riding him as he pushed forward, going deeper, making her climax again. Reaching between them, he cupped her breasts and teased her nipples. She whimpered his name. When he looked at her he found her eyes glazed with passion. His tension increased. He flicked his fingers against her nipples, moving faster until she was panting. His own need became overwhelming. He was trying to make it last, but it was a poorly thought-out plan. With Josie he always lost control.

With one last, deep thrust, he filled her and gave way to the sensation of release. His guttural cry joined hers as they clung to each other through the aftermath of paradise.

Later, much later, when they were both dressed and getting ready to sit down to dinner, Josie looked at him.

"Point well taken," she said with a grin.

"Start with two hours a day," Dr. Sanders said the following week when Josie saw her for her checkup. "Add about an hour a day, but don't push it. You've recovered very nicely. I don't want to see you have another setback."

Josie nodded, feeling both relieved and panicked.

She was being cleared to start using her cane again, albeit slowly. But in a matter of a couple of weeks, she would be back on her feet. Then what?

"I know I was really stupid before," Josie said, smiling at the doctor. "I've learned my lesson. I'll keep up with my physical therapy and do my exercises."

"Don't forget rest. That's important." The doctor glanced at her chart. "It's about time for your next surgery. I believe you're going to have two more. Is that correct?"

Josie nodded. "The good news is by taking it easy these past weeks, I've noticed a real lessening of pain. There are days when I hardly have any. According to my surgeon in Los Angeles, that's only going to get better with the last two surgeries."

"Will you be returning to L.A. for the surgeries or do you want a recommendation for a local physician? I happen to know someone who is very gifted."

Josie hesitated. So many of her plans depended on Del. "I don't know," she admitted. "If I do decide to stay, I'll be in touch."

They shook hands, and Josie wheeled herself from the doctor's office. Her mind raced. Was she staying here in Beachside Bay? Were she and her husband reconciling or just playing house? She knew the best way to get answers was to ask him, but somehow she never managed to find the right moment and the courage at the same time.

Del had been tied up with a client meeting, so Annie May had brought her to her appointment and was waiting in the reception area. The older woman took one look at her face and frowned.

"She didn't give you the all-clear, did she? You look disappointed."

Josie sighed. "No, it was good news. I can start using my cane for a couple of hours a day, building up from there."

Her friend held open the door leading to the corridor. "I don't understand. Shouldn't you look happy?"

"I am, it's just..." She turned at the end of the hall and headed for the elevator. "Now I have to talk to Del. I mean, the only reason I'm living in his house is that I'm in a wheelchair. Once I'm fine, I have no excuse."

Shrewd eyes stared at her. "How about telling him the truth? I'm sure he'd like to know that you're still in love with him."

Josie wasn't surprised that Annie May had guessed her secret. "I've thought about letting him know, but I'm afraid of what he's going to say. I'm not sure how he feels about me. We've talked a little about the past, but not about the present or the future. Maybe this is just a fling for him."

"Del isn't a fling sort of guy."

"What if he's only keeping me around because he feels sorry for me?"

Annie May punched the button for the lobby level and twisted her mouth in disgust. "What if we all turn into flying monkeys? If you're going to worry, worry about something realistic. Del doesn't feel sorry for you."

"Then what does he feel?"

Annie May shrugged. "I don't know. You two need to work that out for yourselves."

The elevator doors opened. Josie propelled herself

toward the parking lot. "What we need is time." She rolled to a stop. "Annie May, would you please not tell him what the doctor said?"

The petite woman walked around to stand in front of Josie. She planted her hands on her hips. "Girl, I am not going to lie for you again."

"Don't lie, just don't tell him the truth."

"Oh, there's a differentiation. No. It's time, Josie. Just come clean. Tell Del you're cleared to start walking and you want to talk about the relationship."

"I'm afraid of giving him an excuse to get rid of me. We're not married anymore. There are no emotional or legal ties. He let me go once, why wouldn't he let me go again? Please, Annie May, just for a couple of weeks. Then I swear I'll tell him myself."

The older woman pressed her lips together. "Damn. I know you're technically divorced, but you've been living together and from what I can guess, sharing a bed. That sounds like marriage to me."

"But it isn't."

"I know."

"Just a couple of weeks. I want to be sure about Del before I give him an excuse to get rid of me."

"That boy is crazy about you. He's not interested in being on his own again." The fiery redhead sighed. "All right. Against my better judgment I'll keep quiet. But only for two weeks. If you haven't come clean by then, I'll tell him myself. You understand me?"

"Yes. Thank you."

Annie May led the way out of the building, grumbling with every step. "I'm just too softhearted for my own good. People are always taking advantage of me. I should know better.''

Josie was too busy with her own thoughts to listen. She had a brief reprieve until it was all going to hit the fan, she thought glumly. Right now she and Del were caught up in a game of playing house. What would happen when the game ended and it was time to get on with their real lives?

Chapter Fifteen

Three days later Josie wheeled herself into the old Miller house. Del had promised her a surprise, so she knew that it was going to look different, but she wasn't prepared for what awaited her inside the freshly stained door.

Fading afternoon light glinted off the newly washed chandelier sparkling overhead in the foyer. To the left was the parlor, converted to a library-sitting room, complete with built-in bookcases. In front of her, the main living area's newly polished floor gleamed. There were new windows, fresh paint and restored moldings.

"I can't believe it," she breathed. "Del, you've done an amazing job."

"It wasn't just me," he said, walking beside her. "The crew worked hard."

"It shows. Everywhere."

She rounded the corner and faced the kitchen. The last time she'd seen it, the room had been gutted. Pipes had jutted out of the walls, and the flooring had looked as if it had been the site of a battle. Now custom cabinets covered three of the four walls. There was a double sink, granite countertops, a center island and a brand-new bay window.

"I love it," she told him.

"Wait until you see the upstairs. We're not done with the master suite, but it's going to be terrific. Give me another week on that, then I'll carry you up to see it."

Josie felt a flash of guilt at Del's words. She was spending nearly three hours a day on her feet, and he didn't know. As far as he was concerned, she was still confined to her wheelchair. She knew she had to come clean and soon, but she was so afraid of what he would say. Did he want her to stay or go?

"I hope you don't have any second thoughts," he said, walking into the kitchen and opening one of the cupboards. He smoothed his hand across the grain of the wood.

"About what?"

"The third floor. Originally you'd wanted it as an exercise room and office."

She grimaced. "That was a long time ago—when we were still fighting about everything from what brand of jam to buy to how to remodel this house. I really liked your plans for the third floor."

He'd wanted the attic converted to a master suite, because he'd wanted the other bedrooms for their children. At the time, Josie hadn't been interested in babies, but she'd changed her mind on that one. She did want children and she wanted them with Del.

If only she could find the courage to ask him to give her a second chance. To give *them* a second chance. But she was scared. She wanted to believe that he didn't mind the changes in her. She wanted to believe he hadn't meant all the things he'd said about her when he'd thought she was Rose, or that if he had meant them, she'd shown him she was different now. But she wasn't sure about any of it. Had they both changed enough to make it work this time?

"I don't say this to be mean," he told her as he closed the cabinet and faced her. "I think it's good we never bought this house."

She knew what he meant. "You're right. Our fighting would have destroyed it. If not physically, then its spirit or whatever it is houses have."

He leaned against the center island. "You're not the only one who has changed, Josie. I'm different, too. I accept my responsibility in what went wrong before. If I could have known what I know now, I would have done it all differently."

What was he saying? "Me, too," she whispered.

"I asked you before what you were going to do about this house. Have you decided?"

She shook her head. If they had a chance of working things out, then she wanted to keep the house for them. If not, she would sell it and go back to Los Angeles. She couldn't stay in Beachside Bay and be close to Del, knowing he would never love her again.

"Are you going to stay in town for a while?" he asked.

That she could answer. She met his direct gaze and nodded. "Yes." He'd asked the question. She forced herself to take the next step. "We're different people today."

"Agreed. Which complicates everything."

How did it complicate anything? she wanted to ask. Damn him for being cryptic. Not that she was being forthcoming, either.

"Maybe we should start with getting to know each other again," she murmured, averting her gaze, then holding her breath.

"I kind of thought we were. Or was that some other wildcat in my bed last night?"

His words made her blush but also eased her tension. "It was me."

He came around the center island to her wheel-chair. "I was teasing," he said. "I'd very much like for us to get to know each other again. If you're willing."

Her heart pounded so loudly, she was sure the neighbors could hear it. "I'd like that very much."

Del stepped into the private cubicle the bank provided for its safety deposit box customers. He sat in the chair and slowly raised the cover on the narrow metal box.

There were several documents, including the pink slips for his truck and his car, a deed to the house and copies of his and his parents' wills. There were also two velvet-covered jewelry boxes.

He opened the first and saw a plain gold man's wedding band. After picking it up, he glanced at the inscription on the inside.

"Be mine forever."

He started to slip the ring onto his left hand, then stopped himself. Instead he put it back in the first box and opened the second. A small diamond solitaire engagement ring winked up at him. There was a matching gold band tucked into the box as well. Josie's rings. She'd returned them to him after she'd left him.

He remembered his pain and shock when he'd opened the envelope. Along with a quitclaim deed, she'd sent back the wedding rings and a check for half their savings account. Right to the bitter end, she'd been more than fair. Although Scott Construction had been in the family for years, his divorce lawyer had warned him that Josie could have requested a portion of profits for the time they were married. He didn't doubt that her lawyer had told her the same. But she'd never once mentioned that. Nor had she asked for anything other than her half of the profit on their house.

He placed her wedding rings into the palm of his hand and squeezed his fingers around the gold and diamonds. A few days before, they'd talked about wanting to get to know each other. Now, holding a piece of their past in his hand, he knew he'd been stalling. He didn't need any more time to know what he wanted. He was in love with her and he wanted to spend the rest of his life with her. He wanted them to get married and this time figure out how to make it work.

He was hopeful, more hopeful than he'd been in a long time. They'd both changed. They had the hard-learned lessons from the past and a second chance. But he also knew the price of what they were doing. There was a whole lot more on the line.

The first time Josie had walked out of his life, he'd been hurt, but he hadn't been destroyed. This time was different. Josie today was an irresistible combination of old and new. Everything he'd adored about her before remained. It blended perfectly with her new traits. Things like patience and honesty. She'd stolen his heart in a whole new way, which meant he was even more at risk. This time if she walked out on him, he wouldn't recover.

The realization didn't change his mind. He needed her in his life. Whatever the risk, he was willing to take it. But not with these.

He put the old rings back into their velvet containers so he could return them to the safety deposit box. He didn't want to start over with these talismans of the past. He was going to propose, and if she accepted, they would wear new rings. Rings that symbolized their future not their past.

Two hours later Del walked into his house. He'd gone to a local jewelry store to look at engagement rings. He'd only planned on window shopping but instead he'd bought a glittering two-carat solitaire that he hoped would leave her breathless. Well, not so breathless that she couldn't say yes.

He was nervous, he admitted to himself. He didn't question that he was doing the right thing. Instead he found himself wondering if Josie would say yes. After all she—

He paused in the center of the living room, noticing for the first time that a pounding beat came from the kitchen. He followed the loud music, not sure what it meant. As he rounded the corner, he saw Josie standing in the center of the kitchen. She was moving in time with the rock music, shifting her weight from hip to hip, singing along.

Dancing!

Walking!

He couldn't believe it. She wasn't in her wheelchair

and she didn't look as if she'd just hopped up for the moment. There was a confidence in her movements, a sureness that indicated not only practice, but lack of pain. He remembered the doctor's visit the week before. Had she been given the all-clear to walk? Why the hell hadn't she told him?

Rage filled him. Once again Josie was playing him for a fool. All this time he'd been planning their future together while she'd been...been... Hell, he didn't know *what* she'd been doing but it was wrong, damn her. This whole thing had been a game. She hadn't changed at all.

He walked over to the radio. She still hadn't seen him. With one violent movement, he turned the knob, shutting off the machine. There was instant silence.

Josie nearly stumbled in surprise. She spun to see what had happened and saw Del standing in the kitchen. He was glaring at her. Something dark and ugly tightened his face. If he'd been any other kind of man she might have worried for her physical safety. Obviously he'd figured out that she was back on her feet, and he wasn't happy about the news. Or rather her silence on the subject.

She felt her legs start to give way. Sudden shock robbed her strength. She made it to one of the kitchen chairs and collapsed. Her chest felt tight, as if she couldn't possibly draw in enough air. Passing out would be a nice touch, she thought, trying to find humor in the situation. Unfortunately Del would probably leave her gasping on the floor. Not that she could blame him. Annie May had warned her, but she hadn't listened. She'd been a coward and now she was paying the price.

"I kept the truth from you before," she said with

a shrug. "One would think I would learn. But I haven't. Not about this. The thing is, my motivation is the same. I was afraid."

It was as if he hadn't heard her. "How long?"

His voice was a low growl. She shivered, but not from pleasure. She understood what he was asking. How long had she been walking?

"Since my last doctor's visit. She told me to start with a couple of hours a day and work up from there."

"And you didn't think I would be interested in that particular piece of information?"

Josie drew in a deep breath. This would be what Annie May liked to call a defining moment in one's life. Fear or no fear, she was going to have to tell him the exact truth, regardless of the consequences. She didn't want to. What if he rejected her? She knew that she would physically survive without Del, but her heart would be small and shattered. Like her legs, it would never fully recover.

What if she'd misunderstood what they were doing? What if—

She shook her head to clear out the doubt. It didn't matter. She *had* to speak the truth from the very depths of her being and hope Del believed her.

Slowly she forced herself to her feet. She moved so that she was behind the chair and could press her hands on the back for support.

"I may not get much better than this," she told him. "I'll have two more surgeries in the next couple of years. They should help, but there's a chance they won't do more than eliminate some of the pain. I might get more mobile, but I might not."

His dark eyes flashed with contempt. "What the hell does that have to do with anything?"

"I want you to be very clear on my condition."

He started to dismiss her with a wave, but she stopped him.

"No," she said forcefully. "Don't brush me off. This is important."

"What's important is why you lied to me. I thought we were making a fresh start. I thought I mattered."

"You do," she said desperately. "Please, Del. Just listen. I'm not who I was three years ago. In some ways that's good, but in others it's not. I haven't fully come to terms with my limitations. I don't think you have, either." She squared her shoulders. "The reason I didn't tell you I was walking was because I didn't want to leave your house. I thought if you knew I was better, you might ask me to go. I didn't know if I would survive that."

"Why would leaving matter?"

He sounded hostile and suspicious. Nothing about his expression told her what he was thinking. It was very possible she was about to make a huge fool of herself, but it was too late for her to stop now.

"I love you, Del. I have for a long time. Maybe I never stopped loving you. Three years ago I was an idiot who walked out on something wonderful. We've been over everything that went wrong between us and this isn't the time to do that again. My point is, I'm sorry for my part in the failure of our marriage."

She was shaking. She shuffled around the chair and sank onto the seat. He was silent, not helping her at all. Still, Josie was determined to get it all out.

"When that truck hit me, I had a couple of seconds before I blacked out. I knew it had been a bad accident, and I really thought I was going to die. I didn't think about my family or my childhood. What I thought about was you. The loss of you and our marriage was my greatest regret. For the past year I've continued thinking about you. That's why I came back. At first I thought it was for closure, but I quickly figured out that I returned because I'm still in love with you.''

He clenched his hands into fists. ''I want to believe you,'' he said desperately.

''Then do. I love you, Del. Worse, I need you. I can't imagine a world without you. I don't want to have to find out, either. I want us to have another chance. You are the best part of me. I need you to survive—not physically, but emotionally. The truth is I've always needed you. I just didn't know it before.''

Something soft and wonderful flickered in his eyes. ''We can't go back to the way it was before. The old Josie and the old Del. It didn't work.''

''I know. We're both different people. It's going to take some effort to avoid old patterns, but I think we're doing really well so far.''

''Me, too.'' He crouched next to her chair. ''The new and improved Josie Scott is the most amazing woman I've ever known.''

Hope flared inside of her. ''Really?''

''Yeah. All I ever wanted was for you to need me.''

''I do need you.''

He took her hand in his. ''I love you, Josie.''

''Oh, Del.''

She threw herself at him. He caught her in his arms and held her close.

''I love you,'' she whispered. ''I'm sorry I didn't tell you I was walking.''

"I know. I even understand. But no more secrets, okay?"

"Promise."

"So you want to get married again, or what."

She straightened. He was smiling at her. "You're proposing?"

"Absolutely. In fact let me do a better job of it."

He shifted so that he was on one knee, then he pulled a ring box out of his pocket and held it out to her.

"I love you, Josie. I want us to start over, learning from the lessons of the past and this time getting it right. I would be very honored if you would agree to be my wife. Again."

She laughed, then hiccupped on an unexpected sob. When he handed her the box, she opened it and stared down at the beautiful diamond ring.

"It's different," she said.

"I still have the old ones, but I thought we deserved something new. For our fresh start. So are you going to marry me?"

Josie hesitated. "I do love you, Del, but I need you to be very sure. I'll never be the same. I have scars."

"You and your scars. What you have, aside from an incredibly stubborn streak, is a man who loves you very much and is grateful to have you back in his life. He would also like you to accept his proposal because the ground is hurting his knee and he wants to take you to bed and make love with you."

She threw her arms around him and laughed. "That was a lovely speech, and I would adore for you to take me to bed."

He kissed her, then slid the ring on her finger. Even as she admired the glittering diamond, he gathered her in his arms and headed for the bedroom. As they entered the room, he murmured, "Say yes, Josie."

"Oh, didn't I accept?"

"Josie!" He growled low in his throat, but this time the tension came from passion, not anger.

"Not just yes, Del," she said just before she kissed him. "But always."

* * * * *

SPECIAL EDITION™

is delighted to present

The Stockwells of Texas

Available January–May 2001

**Where family secrets, scandalous pasts
and unexpected love wreak havoc on the lives
of the infamous Stockwells of Texas!**

THE TYCOON'S INSTANT DAUGHTER
by Christine Rimmer
(SE #1369) on sale January 2001

SEVEN MONTHS AND COUNTING...
by Myrna Temte
(SE #1375) on sale February 2001

HER UNFORGETTABLE FIANCÉ
by Allison Leigh
(SE #1381) on sale March 2001

THE MILLIONAIRE AND THE MOM
by Patricia Kay
(SE #1387) on sale April 2001

THE CATTLEMAN AND THE VIRGIN HEIRESS
by Jackie Merritt
(SE #1393) on sale May 2001

Available at your favorite retail outlet.

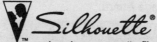

Silhouette®
Where love comes alive™

Visit Silhouette at www.eHarlequin.com   SSESOT

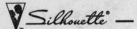

Silhouette® —

where love comes alive—online...

eHARLEQUIN.com

your romantic life

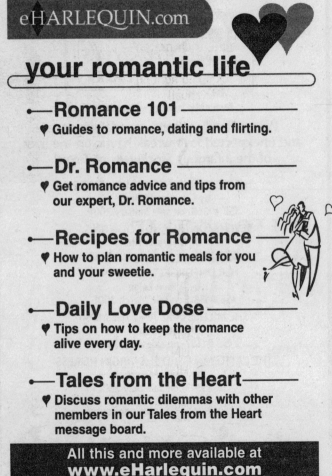

—Romance 101
♥ Guides to romance, dating and flirting.

—Dr. Romance
♥ Get romance advice and tips from our expert, Dr. Romance.

—Recipes for Romance
♥ How to plan romantic meals for you and your sweetie.

—Daily Love Dose
♥ Tips on how to keep the romance alive every day.

—Tales from the Heart
♥ Discuss romantic dilemmas with other members in our Tales from the Heart message board.

All this and more available at
www.eHarlequin.com
on Women.com Networks

SINTL1R

THE Jones GANG

Oggie Jones is at it again!
The wild and woolly Jones gang
are about to meet their match—
in love, that is!
('Cause at feuding and fighting,
they have no equal!)

Marriage— JONES STYLE!

BY

CHRISTINE RIMMER

WAGERED WOMAN
MAN OF THE MOUNTAIN
A HOME FOR THE HUNTER

Come see how it all began—
On sale in retail stores in March 2001

Silhouette®

Where love comes alive™

Visit Silhouette at www.eHarlequin.com

BR3MJ

Every mother wants to see her children marry
and have little ones of their own.

One mother decided to take matters into
her own hands....

Now three Texas-born brothers are about to discover
that mother knows best: A strong man *does* need a
good woman. And babies make a forever family!

Matters of the Heart

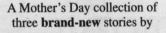

A Mother's Day collection of
three **brand-new** stories by

Pamela Morsi
Ann Major
Annette Broadrick

Available in April at your favorite retail outlets,
only from Silhouette Books!

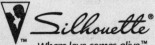

Where love comes alive™

Visit Silhouette at www.eHarlequin.com   PSMOTH

If you enjoyed what you just read,
then we've got an offer you can't resist!

Take 2 bestselling
love stories FREE!
Plus get a FREE surprise gift!

Clip this page and mail it to Silhouette Reader Service™

IN U.S.A.	IN CANADA
3010 Walden Ave.	P.O. Box 609
P.O. Box 1867	Fort Erie, Ontario
Buffalo, N.Y. 14240-1867	L2A 5X3

YES! Please send me 2 free Silhouette Special Edition® novels and my free surprise gift. Then send me 6 brand-new novels every month, which I will receive months before they're available in stores. In the U.S.A., bill me at the bargain price of $3.80 plus 25¢ delivery per book and applicable sales tax, if any*. In Canada, bill me at the bargain price of $4.21 plus 25¢ delivery per book and applicable taxes**. That's the complete price and a savings of at least 10% off the cover prices—what a great deal! I understand that accepting the 2 free books and gift places me under no obligation ever to buy any books. I can always return a shipment and cancel at any time. Even if I never buy another book from Silhouette, the 2 free books and gift are mine to keep forever. So why not take us up on our invitation. You'll be glad you did!

235 SEN C224
335 SEN C225

Name	(PLEASE PRINT)	
Address	Apt.#	
City	State/Prov.	Zip/Postal Code

* Terms and prices subject to change without notice. Sales tax applicable in N.Y.
** Canadian residents will be charged applicable provincial taxes and GST.
All orders subject to approval. Offer limited to one per household.
® are registered trademarks of Harlequin Enterprises Limited.

SPED00   ©1998 Harlequin Enterprises Limited

Beloved author

Sherryl Woods

is back with a brand-new miniseries

The Calamity Janes

**Five women. Five Dreams.
A lifetime of friendship....**

On Sale May 2001—DO YOU TAKE THIS REBEL?
Silhouette Special Edition

On Sale August 2001—COURTING THE ENEMY
Silhouette Special Edition

On Sale September 2001—TO CATCH A THIEF
Silhouette Special Edition

 On Sale October 2001—THE CALAMITY JANES
Silhouette Single Title

On Sale November 2001—WRANGLING THE REDHEAD
Silhouette Special Edition

"Sherryl Woods is an author who writes with a very
special warmth, wit, charm and intelligence."
—*New York Times* bestselling author
Heather Graham Pozzessere

Available at your favorite retail outlet.

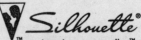

Silhouette®
Where love comes alive™

Visit Silhouette at www.eHarlequin.com
SSETCJ